a hell of
a woman

a hell of
a woman

jim thompson

VINTAGE CRIME / **BLACK LIZARD**

vintage books • a division of random house, inc. • new york

First Vintage Crime/Black Lizard Edition, October 1990

Library of Congress Cataloging-in-Publication Data
Thompson, Jim , 1906–1977.
A hell of a woman/by Jim Thompson—1st Vintage crime/Black Lizard ed.
p.   cm.—(Vintage crime/Black Lizard)
"Bibliography of books by Jim Thompson": p.
ISBN 0-679-73251-9
I. Title.   II. Series.
PS3539.H6733H4   1990
813'.54—dc20   90-50257   CIP

Manufactured in the United States of America
10   9   8   7   6   5   4   3   2   1

a hell of
a woman

I'D GOTTEN out of my car and was running for the porch when I saw her. She was peering through the curtains of the door, and a flash of lightning lit up the dark glass for an instant, framing her face like a picture. And it wasn't a pretty picture, by any means; she was about as far from being a raving beauty as I was. But something about it kind of got me. I tripped over a crack, and almost went sprawling. When I looked up again she was gone, and the curtains were motionless.

I limped on up the steps, set my sample case down and rang the bell. I stepped back from the door and waited, working up a big smile, taking a gander around the yard.

It was a big old-fashioned dwelling, a half-mile or so beyond the state university campus and the only house in that block. Judging by its appearance and location, I guessed that it had probably been a farmhouse at one time.

I punched the bell again. I held my finger on it, listening to its dimly shrill clatter inside the house. I pulled the screen open and began pounding on the door. You did things like that when you worked for Pay-E-Zee Stores. You got used to people who hid when they saw you coming.

The door flew open while I was still beating on it. I took one look at this dame and moved back fast. It wasn't the young one, the haunted-looking babe I'd seen peering through the curtains. This was an old biddy with a beak like a hawk and close-set, mean little eyes. She was about seventy—I don't know how anyone could have got that ugly in less than seventy years—but she looked plenty hale and hearty. She was carrying a heavy cane, and I got the impression that she was all ready to use it. On me.

"Sorry to disturb you," I said, quickly. "I'm Mr. Dillon, Pay-E-Zee Stores. I wonder if—"

"Go 'way," she snarled. "Get out of here! We don't buy from peddlers."

"You don't understand," I said. "Of course, we would like to open an account for you, but what I really stopped by for was some information. I understand you had a Pete Hendrickson working here for you. Did some yard work and so on. I wonder if you could tell me where I can find him."

She hesitated, squinting at me craftily. "He owes you some money, huh?" she said. "You want to find him an' make him pay."

"Not at all," I lied. "It's the other way around, in fact. We accidentally collected too much from him, and we want to—"

"I bet you do!" She let out with an ugly cackle. "I just bet you collected too much from that drunken, lazy bum! No one never got nothing from Pete Hendrickson but a lot of sass and excuses."

I grinned and shrugged. Usually, you had to do it the other way, because it's damned seldom that even a man's worst enemies will tip him off to a bill collector. But once in a while you find someone real low down, someone who just naturally likes to see a guy get it in the neck. And that's the way it was with this old witch.

"Mean and lazy," she said. "Wouldn't do nothing and wanted two prices for doing it. Sneaks off an' gets hisself another job when he's supposed to be workin' for me. I told him he'd be sorry ... "

She gave me Pete's address, also the name of his employer. It was a greenhouse out on Lake Drive, only a few blocks from where I was now, and he'd been working there about ten days. He hadn't made a payday yet, but he was just about due.

"He came whinin' and beggin' around here last night," she said. "Tryin' to borrow a few dollars until he could get his wages. I guess you know what I told him!"

"I can imagine," I said. "Now, as long as I'm here, I'd like to show you some very special items which—"

"Huh-uh! No, sir-ee!" She started to close the door.

"Just let me show them to you," I said, and I stooped down and flipped the sample case open. I laid the stuff out in the lid, talking fast, watching her face for an expression of interest. "What about this spread? Make you a very nice price on that. Or this toilet set? We're practically giving it away, lady. Well, some stockings? A shawl? Gloves? House slippers? If I don't have your size here, I can—"

"Huh-uh. Nope." She wagged her head firmly. "I got no money for such fol-de-rol, mister."

"You don't need any," I said. "Hardly any. Just a very small payment now on any or all of these items, and you can set your own terms on the balance. Take as long to pay as you like."

"I'll bet," she cackled. "Just like Pete Hendrickson, huh? You better go on, mister."

"What about the other lady?" I said. "That other young lady? I'm sure there's something here she'd like to have."

"Huh!" she grunted. "And how do you figger *she'd* pay for anything?"

"I figured she'd probably use money," I said. "But maybe she's got something better."

I was just being snotty, understand. I didn't like her and I'd gotten everything out of her that I was going to get. So why be polite?

I started repacking the stuff, jamming it in any old whichway because that junk was hard to hurt. Then, she spoke again, and there was a sly wheedling note to her voice that brought my head up with a start.

"You like that niece o' mine, mister? You think she's pretty?"

"Why, yes," I said. "I thought she was a very attractive young lady."

"She minds good, too, mister. I tell her to do somethin' and she does it. No matter what."

I said that was swell or fine, or something of the kind. Whatever a guy does say in a situation like that. She pointed down at the sample case.

"That chest of silverware, mister. How much you gettin' on that?"

I opened the chest and showed it to her. I said I really hadn't intended to sell it; it was such a bargain I was saving it for myself. "Service for eight, lady, and every piece of it solid heavy-Sterling plate. We usually get seventy-five dollars for it, but we're closing out these last few sets at thirty-two ninety-five."

She nodded, grinning at me slyly. "You think my niece ... You think she could pay for it, mister? You could fix it up some way so's she could pay for it?"

"Why, I'm sure of it," I said. "I'll have to talk with

her first, of course, but—"

"You let me talk to her first," she said. "You wait here."

She went away, leaving the door open. I lighted a cigarette, and waited. And, no, I'll swear to it on a stack of Bibles, I didn't have any idea of what the old gal was up to. I knew she was pretty low down, but I'd never known many people who weren't. I thought she was acting pretty goofy, but most of Pay-E-Zee's customers were goofs. People with good sense didn't trade with outfits like ours.

I waited, wincing a little when there was a sudden flash of lightning, wondering how many more god-damned days it was going to go on raining. It had been raining for almost three weeks straight, now, and what it had done to my job was murder. Sales way to hell down, collections way to hell off. You just can't do good door-to-door work in rainy weather—you can't get the people to open up. And with accounts like mine, a lot of day laborers and the like, it didn't do much good when they did open up. They'd been laid off on account of the weather. You could cuss them and threaten them, but you just couldn't get what they didn't have.

I was getting fifty a week salary, just about enough to run my car. My earnings had to come from commissions, and I hadn't been pulling down any. Oh, I was making something, sure, but not nearly enough to get by on. I'd kept going by doctoring my accounts, pocketing part of the collections and altering the account-cards accordingly. Right now I was in the hole for better than three hundred dollars, and if someone should squawk before I could square up . . .

I swore under my breath, flipping my cigarette into the yard. I turned back to the door, and there she was—the girl.

She was in her early twenties, I believe, although I'm not the best judge of ages when it comes to women. She had a mass of wavy blonde hair, kind of chopped off rather than bobbed, and her eyes were dark; and maybe they weren't the biggest eyes I'd ever seen on a gal, but in that thin white face they seemed to be.

She was wearing a white wrap-around, the sort of get-up you see on waitresses and lady barbers. The neck of it came down in a deep *V,* and you could see she had plenty of what it takes in that area. But below that, huh-uh. Out around the ag college—I had an account or two out there—the guys would have said she was poor for beef, fine for milk.

She pushed the screen door open. I picked up the sample case, and went in.

She hadn't spoken to me yet, and she didn't now. She'd turned and was walking down the hall almost before I got inside. Walking with her shoulders kind of slumped, as though she were tipping forward. I followed her, thinking maybe she didn't have much there in the rear but there wasn't anything wrong with the shape of it.

We went through the living room, the dining room, the kitchen. Her in the lead, me walking pretty fast to keep up with her. There was no sign of the old woman. The only sound came from our footsteps and the occasional clashes of thunder.

I began to get an uneasy, sickish feeling in the pit of my stomach. If I hadn't needed to make a sale so badly, I'd have walked out.

There was a door leading off the kitchen. She went through it and I followed her—kind of edging around her, keeping my eyes on her. Wanting to say something and not knowing what the hell it would be.

It was a small bedroom; a room with a bed in it, rather, and a washstand with an old-fashioned bowl and pitcher. The shades were drawn, but quite a bit of light seeped in around their edges.

She closed the door and turned her back; started fumbling with the belt of the wrap-around. And I got the pitch then, of course, but it was too damned late. Too late to stop her.

The dress fell to the floor. She had nothing on underneath it. She turned back around.

I didn't want to look. I felt sick and sore and ashamed—and, me, I don't get ashamed easy. But I just couldn't help myself. I had to look, even if I never looked at anything else again.

There was a welt across her like a hot iron might make. Or a stick. Or a cane ... And there was a drop of blood ...

She stood, head bowed, waiting. Her teeth were clenched tightly, but I could see the trembling of her chin.

I said, "God. God, honey ... " And I stooped and picked up the wrap-around. Because I wanted her—I guess I'd wanted her right from the moment I'd seen her at the door, a picture lit up by lightning. But I wouldn't have taken her this way if I'd been paid to.

So I started to get this doohickey back around her, but the way things worked out I didn't quite get the job done. Not right at the moment, anyway. I was fumbling with the damned thing, telling her not to cry, she was a baby girl and a sweet child and I wouldn't hurt her for the world. And finally she looked up into my face, and I guess she must have liked what she saw there as well as I liked what I saw in her.

She leaned into me, snuggled up against me with her head buried against my chest. She put her arms around me, and I put mine around her. We stood there together, holding on to each other for dear life; me patting her on the head and telling her there wasn't a goddamned thing to cry about. Telling her she was a baby girl and a honey child and old Dolly Dillon was going to take care of her.

It seems funny as hell, now that I look back on it. Strange, I mean. Me—a guy like me—in a bedroom with an armful of naked woman, and not even thinking about her being naked. Just thinking about her without thinking about her nakedness.

That's the way it was, though. Exactly the way it was. I'll swear to it on a stack of Bibles.

2

I GOT HER soothed down, finally. I helped her back into the dress and we sat down on the edge of the bed, talking in whispers.

Her first name was Mona, her last was the same as her aunt's, Farrell. So far as she knew, that is. All she had to go on was what the old bitch told her. She couldn't remember living with anyone else. She didn't have any other relatives that she knew of.

"Why don't you clear out?" I said. "She couldn't stop you. She'd get in plenty of trouble if she tried to."

"I ... " She shook her head, vaguely. "I wouldn't know what to do, Dolly. Where to go. I—I just wouldn't know."

"Hell, do anything," I said. "There's plenty of things you could do. Slinging hash. Ushering in a movie. Sales clerking. Housework, if you couldn't find anything else."

"I know, but—but—"

"But what? You can swing it, honey. Don't tell her you're leaving if you don't want to. Just pull out and don't come back. You get out now and then, don't you? She doesn't keep you inside all the time?"

No—yes, she nodded. She got out quite a bit. Downtown and around the neighborhood to shop for the old woman.

"Well, then?" I said.

"I c-couldn't, Dolly ... "

I sighed. I guessed she couldn't either. She was too beat-down, completely lacking in confidence. If there was someone to take her away from here, keep her going until she was built up a little ...

She was looking at me apologetically. Humbly. Begging me with her eyes. I looked down at the floor.

What the hell did she expect me to do, anyway? I was already doing a damned sight more than I should.

"Well," I said, "you'll be all right for the present. I'll leave the silverware here for you. The old girl won't know that—that—she'll lay off of you for a while."

"D-Dolly ... "

"Maybe you'd better make it Frank," I said, trying to steer her away from the important thing. "Dolly"— I laughed at myself. "Now, ain't that a hell of a handle for a big ugly guy like me to have?"

"You're not ugly," she said. "You're pret ... Is that why they call you that? Because you're so—so—?"

"Yeah," I said. "I'm a real pretty guy, I am. Pretty damned tough and ornery, and pretty apt to stay that way."

"You're nice," she said. "I never met anyone who was nice before."

I told her the world was full of nice people. I'd have hated to try to prove it to her, but I said it, anyway. "You'll get along swell, once you're away from here. So why don't you give yourself a break, honey? Let me give you one? I can tell the cops what—"

"No!" She gripped my arm so hard I almost jumped. "No, Dolly! You've got to promise."

"But, baby," I said. "That's all bushwa, she's handed you. They won't do anything to you. She's the one that—"

"No! They wouldn't believe me! She'd say I was lying and she'd make me say it, and a-afterwards—afterwards when she got me alone ... "

Her voice trailed off into terrified silence. I put my arm back around her.

"All right, honey," I said. "I'll think of something else. You just sit tight, and ... " I paused, remembering how quick the old woman had come out with her offer. "Have you had to do anything like this before, Mona? Has she made you?"

She didn't speak, but her head moved up and down. A faint flush spread under the delicate white of her face.

"Just people stopping by, like I did?"

Again a reluctant nod. "M-mostly ... "

That was good, if you know what I mean. Her aunt would pull that on the wrong guy—the right one, rather—and she'd be in the jug, but fast.

"Well, she won't do it any more," I said. "No, I won't give you away. So far as she'll know everything went off per schedule. That's the angle, see? I'll be coming back with plenty of other nice things, and I don't want you bothered."

She raised her head again, and her eyes searched my face. "Will you, Dolly? W-will you come back?"

"Didn't I say so?" I said. "I'll be back, and I'll get you away from here just as soon as I do. It's going to take a little working out, know what I mean? It's kind of complicated the way I'm set up. You see—well, I'm a married man."

She nodded. I was married. So what? It didn't mean anything to her. I guess it wouldn't mean anything, after what she'd been through.

"Yeah," I went on. "Been married for years. And

this job I got, it keeps me humping to make a living."

That didn't register, either. All she knew was that I had a hell of a lot more than she had.

It made me a little sore, the way she was acting, but yet I kind of liked it. She was so damned trusting, so sure that I'd work things out no matter how tough they were. I hadn't had many people believe in me like that. Many? Hell, any.

She smiled at me, shyly, the first time she'd really smiled since I'd met her. She took my hand and moved it over her breast.

"Do you ... want to, Dolly? I wouldn't mind with you."

"Maybe next time," I said. "Right now, I think I'd better be shoving off."

The smile faded. She started to ask me if I minded about the others. I said why would I mind for God's sake, and I gave her a kiss that made her gasp.

Because I did want her, and I wasn't coming back. And when a girl offers you that—all that she has to offer—you ought to be damned careful how you turn it down.

I took the silver chest out of my case, and put it on the dresser. I gave her another kiss, told her not to worry about a thing, and left.

The old hag, her aunt, was in the hallway, grinning and rubbing her hands together. I wanted to bat her in her goddamned rotten puss, but of course I didn't.

"You got something there, lady," I told her. "Take good care of it, because I'm going to be back for more."

She cackled and smirked. "Bring me a nice coat, huh, mister? You got some nice winter coats?"

"I got more coats than you can stack in a barn," I said. "Nothing second hand, get me, and I'm not trading for anything second-hand. I come by here and find someone else in the sack, it's no deal."

"You leave it to me, mister," she said eagerly. "When'll you be back?"

"Tomorrow," I said. "Or maybe the next day. I'm liable to drop by any old time, so don't try any doubling-up on me if you want that coat."

She promised she wouldn't.

I opened the door, and ran back down the walk to my car.

It was still pouring down rain. It looked like it was going to rain forever. And I owed the company another thirty-three dollars. Thirty-two ninty-five to be exact.

"You're doing swell, Dolly," I told myself. "Yes, sir, Dillon, you're doing all right . . . You think this Staples character is stupid? You think that's how he got the job of checking on characters like you? You think he ain't the meanest, toughest son-of-a-bitch in the Pay-E-Zee chain?"

Goddamn, I thought. Double goddamn and a carton of hells.

Then, I shoved my car into gear and got going. It was only four-thirty. I had plenty of time to get out to the greenhouse and see Pete Hendrickson before he knocked off for the day.

And if Pete wasn't a real good boy . . .

Suddenly, I grinned to myself. Grinned and scowled at the same time . . . He'd gotten to that poor damned girl, Mona; I'd have bet money on it. The old woman would have tried to pay him off that way, and Pete wouldn't have turned it down. He'd let his bills go to hell—let me chase all over town hunting for him—and do *that* to her. And even if he hadn't he was still no good.

And I needed every nickle of what he owed us.

I parked in front of the greenhouse, in front of the

office, that is. I reached into the pocket of the car, took out a sheaf of papers and thumbed through them rapidly.

I found his sales contract—a contract that was also an assignment of wages. You had to look for it a little because of the fine print, but it was there all right. All legal and air-tight.

I took it into the office, and presented it to Pete's boss. He paid off like a slot machine. Thirty-eight bucks and not a word of argument. He counted it out to me, and then I recounted it, and while I was still standing there he told a clerk to go and get Pete.

I finished the count fast, and beat it.

Wage assignments and garnishees—employers just naturally don't like the things. They don't like to be bothered with them, and they don't like employees who cause them to be bothered. Pete was going to get the gate. I figured I'd better be some place else when he did.

I drove down the street a few blocks to a beer joint. I ordered a pitcher of beer, carried it back to a rear booth and took down half of it at a gulp. Then, I spread a blank contract out on the table, and made out a cash sale to Mona Farrell for thirty-two ninety-five.

That was one thing off my mind. That took care of the silver, with five bucks left over. Now, if this rain would only stop and I could get in a few good weeks in a row ...

I began to feel a little better. Not quite so damned blue and hopeless. I ordered another pitcher of beer, sipping it slowly this time. I thought what a sweet kid that Mona was, and I wondered why I couldn't have married her instead of a goddamned bag like Joyce.

That Joyce. Now, there was a number for you. Kid Sloppybutt, Princess Lead-in-the-Tail, Queen of the

Cigarette Girls and a free pinch with every pack. I'd thought she was hot stuff, but it hadn't been recently, brother. I may have been stupid to begin with, but I wised up fast. Joyce—a lazy, selfish dirty slob like Joyce for a wife.

Why couldn't it have been Mona?

Why was it that every time I thought I was getting a break it went sour on me?

I glanced at the clock. Ten minutes of six. I stepped to the telephone, and dialed the store.

Staples sounded just the same as usual. Smooth, oily, soft-voiced. I told him I was chasing a skip through the sticks, and I thought I'd wait until morning to check in.

"Quite all right, Frank," he said. "How's it going, anyway? Any lead yet on Hendrickson?"

"Nothing yet," I lied, "but I've had a fairly good day. I made a cash sale on that silver special."

"Good boy," he said. "Now, if you can just get a line on Hendrickson."

His voice lingered over the name. Underlined it. He was more than five miles away, but I felt like he was right there. Grinning at me, watching me, waiting for me to trap myself.

"What about it, Frank?" he said. "What about that thirty-eight dollars Hendrickson owes us?"

3

"WHAT THE HELL you think I've been doing?" I said. "I haven't been sitting around on my can in some nice dry office all day. Give me a little time, for God's sake."

The phone was silent for a moment. Then he laughed softly.

"Not too much time, Frank," he said. "Why not put in a little extra effort, eh, as long as you're working over? Use that shrewd brain of yours. I can't tell you how delighted I'd be if you could bring that Hendrickson money in the morning."

"Well, that makes two of us," I said. "I'll do the best I can."

I said goodnight, and hung up the receiver. I drank the rest of my beer, not enjoying it very much.

Had he been giving me a hint, a warning? Why was he bearing down so hard on this one account? Hendrickson was a dead beat, sure, but practically all of our customers were. They seldom paid unless they were made to. They traded with us because they couldn't get credit anywhere else. Why, with at least a hundred other skips and no-pays to pick on, had Staples jumped me about this one?

I didn't like it. It might be the beginning of the end,

the first step toward the jailhouse. Because if he caught me tapping one account, he'd figure I'd tapped the others. He'd check on all the others.

Of course, he'd done things like this before. Kind of like this. You'd knock yourself out and have a pretty good day maybe, and instead of a pat on the head you'd get what I'd got tonight. You know. Maybe you've worked for guys like that. They just slide over what you've done, and needle you about something else. The first damned thing that pops into their minds. That has to be done, too, and what the hell are you waiting on?

So . . . so that must be it, I decided. I hoped that was it. You couldn't satisfy Staples. The more you did the more you had to do.

I went up to the bar and paid my check. I walked to the door and looked out into the rain. Turning up my coat collar. Getting ready to make a run for my car.

Night was setting in early, but it wasn't quite dark yet. I could see pretty good, and I saw him down near the end of the building. A big husky guy in work clothes, standing back under the eaves of the building.

I couldn't get to my car without passing him.

I guessed I'd stopped a little too close to that greenhouse.

I went back to the bar, and ordered a quart of beer to take out. Gripping it by the neck, I sauntered out the door.

Maybe he didn't see me right away. Or maybe he was just trying to work his nerve up. Anyway, I was almost parallel with him before he moved out from under the eaves and placed himself in front of me.

I stopped and backed up a step or two.

"Why, Pete," I said. "How's it going, boy?"

"You sonabitch, Dillon," he said. "You get my chob,

hah? You get chob, now I get you!"

"Oh, now, Pete," I said. "You brought it on yourself, fellow. We trust you and try to treat you nice, and you—"

"You lie! Chunk you sell me. Suit no good—like paper it vears! In chail you should be, chunk seller, t'ief, robber! A fine chob I get, and because I no pay for chunk, you—you—I fix you, Dillon!"

He lowered his head, clubbed his big hands into fists. I moved back another step, tightened my grip on the bottle. I was carrying it back behind my thigh. He hadn't seen it yet.

"Jail, huh?" I said. "You've hit a few jails yourself, haven't you, Pete? You keep on fooling around with me and you'll land in another one."

It was just a guess, but it stopped him for a moment. You couldn't go very far wrong in guessing that a Pay-E-Zee customer had made the clink.

"So!" he sputtered. "In chail I haf been, and my time I serve. Dot has nodding to do mit dis. You—"

"What about a sentence for rape?" I said. "Spit it out, goddamn you! Tell me you didn't do it! Tell me you didn't have that poor, sick, starved-to-death kid!"

I moved in on him, not giving him a chance to deny it. I knew damned well that he had and it made me half-crazy to think about it. "Come on, you ugly, overgrown son-of-a-bitch," I said. "Come on and get it!"

And he came on with a rush.

I sidestepped, swinging the bottle like a bat. My feet slipped in the mud. I caught him squarely across the bridge of the nose, and he went down sprawling. But his right fist got me as he went by. It landed, skidding, just below my heart. And if I hadn't bounced back against the building I'd have gone down with him.

I was doubled up for a moment, feeling like I'd never breathe again. Then, I got pulled together a little, and I staggered over to where he was.

He wasn't completely out, but there wasn't any more fight in him. There was no sense in socking him again or giving him a kick in the head. I grabbed him by the collar and dragged him over against the side of the building. I propped him up so that he was kind of out of the rain and wouldn't get run over. And then I knocked the beer open on a rock and pushed it into his hand.

It wasn't the kind of treatment he'd expected. Or was used to. He looked up at me like a beaten dog. On an impulse—or maybe it was a hunch—I took five ones from my pocket and dropped them into his lap.

"I'm sorry about the job," I said. "Maybe I can turn up another one for you ... Like to have me do that? Let you know if I hear of anything?"

He nodded slowly, brushing the blood away from his nose. "I like, yess. B-but—but *vy*, Dillon? Mis-ter Dillon. Vy you do dis an' den you do—"

"No choice," I shrugged. "The company says get the money, I have to get it. You say you want to fight, I fight. When I have my own way, well, you can see for yourself. I treat you like a long-lost brother. Give you dough out of my own pocket, try to find another job for you."

He took a drink of the beer; took another one. He belched and shook his head.

"Iss badt," he said. "Vy you do it. Mis-ter Dillon? Soch a nice man, vy you vork for bad peoples?"

I told him he had me there: I guessed I was just such a nice guy that people took advantage of me. Then, I told him to take it easy, and headed for home.

My ribs ached like hell, and I couldn't get Staples off

my mind. But in spite of the pain and the worry, I laughed out loud ... What a character! If people kept on telling me I was a nice guy, I might start believing them. And yet—well, what was so damned funny about that? What the hell was there to laugh about?

I'd never hurt anyone if I could get out of it. I'd given plenty of people breaks when I didn't have to. Like today for example; just take today, now. Pretty good, huh? You're damn well right it was! How many other guys would have passed up Mona, and given a hand to a guy who'd tried to murder 'em?

Pete had the right dope. It wasn't me, but the job. And I didn't know how to get out of it, any more than I knew how I'd got into it. I—

Did you ever think much about jobs? I mean, some of the jobs people land in? You see a guy giving haircuts to dogs, or maybe going along the curb with a shovel, scooping up horse manure. And you think, now why is the silly bastard doing that? He looks fairly bright, about as bright as anyone else. Why the hell does he do that for a living?

You kind of grin and look down your nose at him. You think he's nuts, know what I mean, or he doesn't have any ambition. And then you take a good look at yourself, and you stop wondering about the other guy ... You've got all your hands and feet. Your health is okay, and you make a nice appearance, and ambition—man! you've got it. You're young, I guess you'd call thirty young, and you're strong. You don't have much education, but you've got more than plenty of other people who go to the top. And yet with all that—with all you've had to do with—this is as far as you've got. And something tells you, you're not going much farther if any.

And there's nothing to be done about it now, of

course, but you can't stop hoping. You can't stop wondering ...

... Maybe you had too much ambition. Maybe that was the trouble. You couldn't see yourself spending forty years moving up from office boy to president. So you signed on with a circulation crew; you worked the magazines from one coast to another. And then you ran across a nice little brush deal—it sounded nice, anyway. And you worked that until you found something better, something that looked better. And you moved from that something to another something. Coffee-and-tea premiums, dinnerware, penny-a-day insurance, photo coupons, cemetery lots, hosiery, extract, and God knows what all. You begged for the charities. You bought the old gold. You went back to the magazines and the brushes and the coffee and tea. You made good money, a couple of hundred a week sometimes. But when you averaged it up, the good weeks with the bad, it wasn't so good. Fifty or sixty a week, well, maybe seventy. More than you could make, probably, behind a gas pump or a soda fountain. But you had to knock yourself out to do it, and you were just standing still. You were still there at the starting place. And you weren't a kid any more.

So you come to this town, and you see this ad. Man for outside sales and collections. Good deal for hard worker. And you think maybe this is it. This sounds like a right job; this looks like a right town. So you take the job, and you settle down in the town. And, of course, neither one of 'em is right, they're just like all the others. The job stinks. The town stinks. You stink. And there's not a goddamned thing you can do about it.

All you can do is go on like those other guys go on.

23

The guy giving haircuts to dogs, and the guy sweeping up horse manure. Hating it. Hating yourself.
  And hoping.

4

WE LIVED in a little four-room dump on the edge of the business district. It wasn't any choice neighborhood, know what I mean? We had a wrecking yard on one side of us and a railroad spur on the other. But it was choice enough for us. We were as well off there as we would be anywhere. A palace or a shack, it always worked out to the same difference. If it wasn't a dump to begin with, it damned soon got to be.

All it took was for us to move in.

I went inside, taking off my coat and hat. I laid them down on my sample case—at least *it* was clean—and took a look around. The floor hadn't been swept. The ash trays were loaded with butts. Last night's newspapers were scattered all over. The ... hell, nothing was as it should be. Nothing but dirt and disorder wherever you looked.

The kitchen sink was filled with dirty dishes; there were soiled sticky pans all over the stove. She'd just got through eating, it looked like, and of course she'd left the butter and everything else sitting out. So now the roaches were having themselves a meal. Those roaches really had a happy home with us. They got a hell of a lot more to eat than I did.

I looked in the bedroom. It looked like a cyclone had

25

struck it. A cyclone and a dust storm.

I kicked the bathroom door open, and went in.

It was one of her good days, I guess. Here it was only seven o'clock at night and she'd actually got some clothes on. Not many; just a garter belt and some shoes and stockings. But that was damned good for her.

She drew a lipstick over her mouth, squinting at me in the medicine cabinet mirror.

"Well," she drawled, "if it isn't the king! And just as polite as ever, too."

"Okay," I said. "You can hop back into your nightgown. I've seen you before, and I still say there's better ones on sidewalks."

"Oh-yeah?" Her eyes flashed. "You rotten bastard! When I think of all the good guys I passed up to marry you, I—"

"Passed them up?" I said. "You mean lined 'em up, don't you?"

"You're a goddamned liar! I n-never—" She dropped the lipstick into the sink, and whirled around facing me. "Dolly," she said. "Oh, Dolly, hon! What's the matter with us?"

"Us? What do you mean, us?" I said. "I'm out knocking myself out every day. I work my can off, and what the hell do I get for it? Not a goddamn thing, that's what. Not even a decent meal or a clean bed, or even a place where I can sit down without a lot of cockroaches swarming all over me."

"I—" She bit her lip. "I know, Dolly. But they just keep coming back, those insects, no matter what I do. And I can just work from morning until night and this place always looks the same. And, well, I guess I just get tired, Dolly. There doesn't seem to be any sense to it. There's nothing here to work with. The sink keeps stopping up, and there's big cracks in the floor and—"

"So what about the other places we've lived? I guess you kept them all clean and pretty?"

"We've never lived in a really nice place, Dolly. Any place where I had a chance. It's always been some dump like this one."

"You mean they got to be dumps," I said. "After you lazed and loafed around and let everything go to hell. You just don't give a damn, that's all. Why, dammit, you should have seen what my mother had to work with—how nice she kept the place we lived in. Seven kids in an east side coldwater tenement, and everything was as shiny and spotless—"

"All right!" she yelled. "But I'm not your mother! I'm not some other woman! I'm me, get me? Me, me!"

"And you're bragging about it?" I said.

Her mouth opened and closed. She gave me a long slow look, and turned back to the mirror.

"Okay," I said. "Okay. You're a princess charming, and I'm a heel. I know you don't have it easy. I know it would be a lot better if I made more money, and I wish to God I could. But I can't and I can't help it. So why not make the best of things as they are?"

"I'm through talking," she said. "I might have known it was no use."

"Goddammit," I said, "I'm apologizing. I've been out in the rain all day while you were lying in the sack, and I come home to a goddamned pig pen and I'm sick and tired and worried, and—"

"Sing 'em," she said. "Sing 'em, king."

"I said I was sorry!" I said. "I apologize. Now, what about chasing your pets out of the grub and fixing me some supper?"

"Fix your own damned supper. You wouldn't like anything I fixed."

She laid down the lipstick and picked up an eyebrow pencil. A crazy, blinding pain speared through my forehead.

"Joyce," I said. "I said I was sorry, Joyce. I'm asking you to please fix me some supper, Joyce. Please, understand? Please!"

"Keep on asking," she said. "It's a pleasure to refuse."

She went on making with the eyebrow pencil. You'd have thought I wasn't there.

"Baby," I said, "I'm telling you. I'm kidding you not. You better drag tail into that kitchen while it's still fastened onto you. You screw around with me a little more and you'll have to carry it in a satchel."

"Now, aren't you sweet?" she said.

"I'm warning you, Joyce. I'm giving you one last chance."

"All hail the king." She made a noise with her lips. "Here's a kiss for you, king."

"And here's one for you," I said.

I brought it up from the belt, the sweetest left hook you ever saw in your life. She spun around on her heels and flopped backwards, right into the tub full of dirty bath water. And, Jesus, did it make a mess out of her.

I leaned against the door, laughing. She scrambled out of the tub, dripping with that dirty soapy scum, and reached for a towel. I hadn't really hurt her, you know. Why hell, if I'd wanted to give her a full hook I'd taken her head off.

She began drying herself, not saying anything at first, and I kind of stopped laughing. Then, she said something that was funny as hell, and yet it was kind of sad. She said it sort of thoughtful and soft-voiced, as though it was the most important thing in the world.

"That was my last good pair of stockings, Dolly. You ruined my only pair of stockings."

"Aah, hell," I said. "I'll give you another pair. I've got some in my sample case."

"I can't wear those. They never fit around the heel. I guess I'll just have to go barelegged."

"Go?" I said.

"I'm leaving. Now. Tonight. I don't want anything from you. I can pawn my watch and my ring—get enough to get by on until I land a job. All I want is to get away from here."

I told her all right, if she wanted to be stupid: those number fives of hers weren't nailed to the floor. "But I think you ought to mull it over a little first. You ought to stick around, anyway, until you run across a job. You know there's no nightclubs in a burg like this."

"I'll find something. There's no law that says I have to stay in this town."

"Why the hell didn't you get a job before this?" I said. "If you'd ever contributed anything, tried to help out a little—"

"Why should I? Why should I want to? I should get out and work for a guy that couldn't even say a nice word in church?" Her voice rose and went down again. "All right, Dolly, I said it all a while ago. I'm me, not someone else. Maybe I should have done a lot of things and maybe you should have, but we didn't and we wouldn't if we had it to do over again. Now, if you'll excuse me . . . let me get cleaned up a little . . . "

"Why so damned modest all of a sudden?" I said. "We're still married."

"We won't be any longer that I can help it. Will you please leave, now, Dolly?"

I shrugged and started out the door. "Okay," I said.

"I'm going downtown and get some chow. Good luck and my best regards to the boys on the vice squad."

"D-Dolly ... is that all you can say at a time like this?"

"What do you want me to say? Peter, Peter, Pumpkin Eater?"

"D-don't you ... Would you like to kiss me good-bye?"

I jerked my head at the mirror. "That?" I said. "Three guesses, toots, and the secret word is still no."

I went on out, turning my back like a damned fool; and the next thing I knew a scrubbing brush socked me in the skull. It hurt like hell, and the dirty names she was yelling at me didn't exactly help it. But I didn't sock her any more, or even curse back at her. I'd said enough, I guessed. I'd done enough.

I loaded my sample case into the car, and took off for town.

I killed a couple hours, eating and doctoring my account cards, and went back home.

She was gone but her memory lingered on, if you know what I mean. She'd left me something to remember her by. The bedroom windows were pushed up to the top, and the bed was soaked with rain. My clothes—well, I just didn't have any clothes.

She'd poured ink all over my shirts. She'd taken a pair of scissors and cut big holes in my suit, the only other suit I had. My neckties and handkerchiefs were snipped to pieces. All my socks and underwear were stuffed into the toilet.

A real swell kid, didn't I tell you? A regular little doll. I'd have to do something nice for her if I ever ran into her again.

I went to work, straightening things out the best I could, and it must have been two in the morning before I got through and stretched out on the lounge.

Worn out, burned up, wondering. I just couldn't get it, you know. Why, if she didn't like a guy and didn't want to get along with him, had she gone to so damned much trouble to get him?

I'd met her in Houston about three years ago. I was crew manager on a magazine deal, and she was pushing cigarettes in this dive; and I used to drop in for a ball every night or so. Well, she started playing for me right from the beginning. The way she hung over my table you'd have thought she was the cloth. I couldn't lift a drink without seeing her through the bottom of the glass. So—so one thing led to another, and I began taking her home from work. What's a guy going to do, anyway, when a chick keeps throwing herself at him? I left her at her door a few nights, and then she let me come inside. And she had one of the nicest little efficiency apartments you ever saw. I guess they had maid service in this joint, and with just herself to look after she got by pretty good. Not that I made any inspection of the place. I had my mind on something else. So I said, howsa about it, honey, and—*boing!* She hauled off and slapped me in the kisser. I jumped up and started to leave. She started crying. She said I wouldn't think she was a nice girl if she did; I wouldn't want to marry her and I'd throw it up to her afterwards. And I said, Aw, now, honey. What kind of a guy do you—

No, now wait a minute! I think I'm getting this thing all fouled up. I believe it was Doris who acted that way, the gal I was married to before Joyce. Yeah, it must have been Doris—or was it Ellen? Well, it doesn't make much difference; they were all alike. They all turned out the same way. So, as I was saying: I said, What kind of a guy do you think I am? And she said ... they said ... I think you're nice. I—

... I went to sleep.

5

PAY-E-ZEE had seventy-five stores across the country. I'll tell you about this one, the one I worked for, and you'll know about them all.

It was on a side street, a twelve-foot-front place between a shine parlor and a fruit stand. It had two small show windows, with about a hundred items in each one. Men's suits, women's dresses, work clothes, bathrobes, wristwatches, dresser sets, novelties— more stuff than I can name. Why it was there, I don't know, because it wasn't once in a month of Saturdays that we got a customer off the street. Practically all the selling was done on the outside by me and five other guys.

We did a volume of about fifteen grand a month, with collections running about seventy-five per cent. And, yeah, that's low all right, but our mark-up wasn't. With a mark-up of three hundred per cent you can take a big loss on collections. You'll still do better on a fifteen-g volume than most stores do on fifty.

I was a little late getting in that morning, and the other collector-salesmen were already gone. A heavy-set guy—a "just looking" customer—was thumbing through the rack of men's jackets. Staples was in the office at the rear, a space separated from the rest of the store by a wall-to-wall counter.

Pay-E-Zee didn't have the usual office employees. Just the credit men-managers like Staples. I laid out my collection cards and cash on the counter and he checked one against the other.

He was a little guy of about fifty, gray-haired, paunchy, sort of baby-mouthed. Back in the days when he was ringing doorbells, they'd called him The Weeper. He'd get on some poor bastard's doorstep or maybe call on him on the job, and then he'd howl and cry and carry on until they could hear him in the next county. He wasn't up to the rough stuff, so he'd pull that. And they'd have to come across to get rid of him.

He talked kind of sissified, not with a lisp, exactly, although you kept expecting one. He finished the check, and smiled at me pleasantly. He removed his glasses, polished them slowly and put them back on again.

"Frank," he said. "I'm disappointed in you. Very, very disappointed."

"Yeah?" I said. "What's the beef now?"

"Such clumsiness, Frank. Such preposterous ineptness. We did things much better in my day. Why in the world didn't you steal from the profit and loss file—the inactive p. and l.'s? If you were at all clever, you might have got away with it for years."

He shook his head sadly, looking like he was about to cry.

I forced a laugh. "Steal? What the hell you handing me, Staples?"

"Oh, Frank, please!" He held up a hand. "You're making this very painful. Pete Hendrickson's employer called me yesterday; his ex-employer, I should say. It seems that he wasn't very favorably impressed with our way of doing business, and he felt constrained to tell me so."

"So what?" I said.

"Frank ... "

"All right," I said. "I borrowed thirty-eight bucks. I'll have it back for you by the end of the week."

"I see. And what about the rest of it?"

"What rest?" I said. "Who you trying to crap, anyway?"

But I knew it was no use. He sighed and shook his head, looking at me sorrowfully.

"I've only had time to spot check your accounts, Frank, but I've already found a dozen—uh—defalcations. Why not get it off your chest, my boy? Give me the total amount of the shortage. I'll find out, anyway."

"I couldn't help it," I said. "It was the rain. It's cleared up now, and if you'll just give me a few weeks—"

"How much, Frank?"

"I've got it all written down." I took out my notebook and showed him. "You can see for yourself I was going to pay it back. Hell, if I didn't intend to pay it back I wouldn't have written it down, would I?"

"We-el, yes." He pursed his lips. "Yes, I think you would have. I know I would have. It looks much better in such unpleasant eventualities as the present one."

"Now, wait a minute," I said. "I—"

"Three hundred and forty-five dollars, eh? Why don't you just dig it up, like a good boy, and we'll consider the matter closed."

"I'll write you a check," I said. "For God's sake, Staples, if I had any money or if I'd been able to beg or borrow any, I wouldn't have taken this."

"Mmm. I suppose so. What about your car?"

"Who's got a car? Talk to the finance company."

"Furniture?"

"Nothing. I rent furnished. I'm telling you, Staples, I don't have it and there's no way I can get it. All I can do is—"

"I see," he said. "Well, that's certainly too bad, isn't it? Very depressing. The company isn't at all vindictive in these matters, but ... I suppose you're familiar with the law of this state? Anything over fifty dollars is grand larceny."

"Look," I said. "What's that going to make you? What the hell good is it going to do to have me slapped in jail? God, if you'll just—"

"Well, it might do quite a bit of good," he said. "A man faced with a long prison sentence often thinks of resources he's previously overlooked. That's been our experience."

"But I can't! I won't!" I said. "There's no one that will help me. I haven't seen any of my relatives in years and they're all poor as hell anyway. I don't have any close friends or—"

"What about your wife?"

"I'm telling you," I said. "There's just one way I can get that dough. Give me six weeks. Give me a month. Three weeks. I'll work seven days a week, sixteen hours a day until—You've got to, Staples! Just a few weeks, a—"

"Oh, I couldn't do that, Frank!" He shook his head firmly. "I'd love to, but I honestly couldn't ... Officer!"

"For God's sake—*Officer?*"

It was the guy I'd thought was a "just looking" customer. He sauntered up behind me, a toothpick bobbling in the corner of his mouth, and gripped me by the elbow.

"Okay, Buster," he said. "Let's go bye bye."

Staples beamed at him. He smiled at me. "I can't bear to say good-bye, Frank. Shall we just make it *au revoir?*"

6

IT MAY SOUND funny, but it was the first time in my life I'd been in jail. That's the God's truth, and I'm kidding you not. I'd crisscrossed the country, been in every state in the union at one time or another; and some of the deals I'd worked were as raw as a tack-factory whore. But I'd never made the can. Guys all around me did. Guys working right across the street from me. But never me. I guess I just don't look like a guy who'd get out of line. I may talk and act that way, but I don't look it. And I don't, if you know what I mean, really feel it.

It was about ten o'clock in the morning by the time they got me booked and locked up. I looked around the tank, the bullpen, and I'm not snobbish or anything, you understand, but I went over in a corner and sat down by myself. I just couldn't take it, somehow. I couldn't believe that I was part of this, that I was in the same boat with these other guys and a lot worse off maybe. Me, old Dolly Dillon, in the jug on a grand larceny rap? It was crazy. I felt like I was dreaming.

I knew better, but all that day I kept thinking that Staples would soften up. He'd realize that I couldn't raise anything in here, and he'd withdraw the charge and let me work the debt off. I kept thinking that, hoping it, and I figured out just the proposition I'd make him. My rent was paid for the month, and I was paid up with the finance company. So I'd say, Okay, Staples, here's what I'll do with you. You buy me a few meal tickets and pay for my gas and oil, and everything over that ...

I remembered that the store owed me money. Two—two-and-a-half day's wages if they'd allow a half for this morning. So, hell, there was twenty-five dollars right there. All I actually owed was, well, call it three hundred in round numbers. That wasn't any money, for God's sake! I could make it up in no time, now that Joyce had pulled out.

I knew Staples would get me out. I mean, I *knew* it.

And I guess you know he didn't.

The next day came and passed. And I began to think about other angles, other ways I'd get out. They were all as hopeless as the Staples deal, but I dreamed up one after another. Maybe some crew would hit town, and they'd know what I could do, and they'd all take up a collection—they'd find out where I was some way—and ... Or maybe I had a big bonus coming from one of the companies I'd worked for and the check was just now catching up with me. Or maybe one of my kinfolks back east had passed on and I was down for the insurance. Or maybe Doris would pop up with a roll. Or Ellen. Or—or someone. Someone had to, dammit! Something had to happen.

No one did, nothing did. And it was hard to take, brother, but it finally sank in on me that that was the way it was going to be. I was stuck. I couldn't kid myself any longer.

I thought about Mona, how she was really the cause of the whole trouble. If I hadn't used Pete Hendrickson's money to pay for that silverware, Staples wouldn't have caught up with me. I called myself all kinds of a damned fool, and I cussed her a little, too, I guess. But I didn't really have my heart in it. I knew I'd have done the same thing all over again, and I wasn't sore at her that much. How could you be sore at a sweet, helpless kid like that?

I sat off by myself in a corner of the bullpen, thinking about her and getting a nice warm feeling. She'd come right to me that day. Put her arms around me and laid her head against my chest. She'd stood there naked and shivering. And she'd hugged me tighter and tighter until I seemed to be part of her.

She was out of this world, that little girl. Not one of these goddamned tramps like I was always latching onto. You could really go places with a kid like that. You'd do anything in the world for her because you knew she'd do anything in the world for you, and you could just naturally go to town.

I wondered what she'd think when I didn't come back. I wondered what would happen to her. I closed my eyes, and I could almost see it happening: the guys coming there to the door and the old woman propositioning them, and Mona ... Mona there in the bedroom ...

I opened my eyes fast. I forced my mind away from her, and started thinking about that house.

I'd had a feeling about it from the moment I set foot inside the door; that it wasn't as it should be, you know. I couldn't figure out what it was at the time, and I'd had plenty of other things to think about afterwards.

But now it finally came to me. There weren't any pictures in the place; pictures of people, I mean.

I guess I've probably been in ten thousand of those old houses, places occupied by old people. And everyone

a hell of a woman

of 'em's got a flock of pictures on the walls. Guys with beards and gates-ajar collars. Women in high-necked dresses with leg-of-mutton sleeves. Boys in Buster Brown suits, and girls in middies and bloomers. Grandpa Jones, Uncle Bill and Aunt Hattie. Cousin Susie's kids ... All those old houses are like that. They've all got those pictures. But this one didn't have a damned one.

I kept turning it over in my mind, and finally I thought, So what? What's it to you, anyway? I got kind of sore at myself, you know, thinking about a thing like that in the spot I was in. So I forgot about it, went back to worrying about myself, and it was days before I thought of it again. And by that time—

I don't know. You'll have to decide for yourself. Maybe any time would have been too late.

Maybe it would have turned out the same way, anyway ... I went to jail on Wednesday morning. I was scheduled for arraignment Friday afternoon. The turnkey came around at two that day, and took me to the showers. I bathed and shaved while he stood and watched, and then he gave me my clothes.

I got dressed. He led me up a long corridor, through a lot of gates, to the receiving room. He gave my name to the cop behind the desk. The cop opened a drawer, thumbed through a bunch of envelopes and tossed one on the counter.

"Open it up," he said. "Anything's missing, you say so now."

I opened it up. My wallet was in it and my car keys and a check to the police parking lot.

"Okay?" he said. "Well, put your John Hancock on this."

I signed a receipt. I thought this was a screwy way to do things, put a guy through all this just to go before a judge. But like I say, I'd never been in jail, and I figured they ought to know what they were doing.

I put the stuff in my pocket. The door to the street was open, and I thought, man oh man, what wouldn't I give to be out there.

The turnkey had gone back behind the counter. He was over at the water cooler, rinsing his mouth out and spitting into a big brass gaboon. He seemed to have forgotten all about me. I stood and waited.

Finally, the desk cop looked up at me. "You like this place, Mac?"

"I guess I got to like it," I said.

"Beat it," he said. "What the hell you waiting on? You got all your junk, ain't you?"

"Yes, sir," I said. "Think you kindly, sir!" And I went out of that damned place so fast, I bet I didn't even cast a shadow.

I was sure it was a mistake, see? They had me mixed up with some other guy. I didn't see how it could be any other way.

I got my car off the parking lot. I came off of it like a bat out of hell, and I must have gone four or five blocks before I came to my senses and slowed down.

This wasn't going to get it. How far did I think I'd go with a finance-company car and a little over two bucks? Maybe the cops had pulled a boner, and maybe Staples had decided to give me a break. Either way I couldn't lose by seeing him. If this was on the level, swell. If not, that was swell too. At least I could beat his rotten tail off before I went back to jail.

I parked a few doors below the store. I sidled up to the window, and glanced through the door.

He was about halfway down the aisle, counting stock, it looked like. His back to me.

I jerked the door open fast, and went in. He started,

and whirled around.

He came toward me, swiftly, hand extended.

"My dear boy! I'm so glad they released you promptly. I asked them not to take a moment longer than was necessary. I made it very urgent, Frank."

"Well, okay," I said. "I'm not kicking, understand. But you ask me, three days isn't very damned prompt."

"But, Frank." He spread his hands. "It wasn't three days. It was hardly an hour ago that your wife repaid the money."

MY WIFE? A wife I didn't really have, now, had ponied up the dough? Hell, she couldn't have. She wouldn't have if she could.

Staples looked at me expectantly. "You mean to say you didn't know? She didn't tell you she was arranging your release?"

There was a purring, pleased note to his voice. I didn't know what the situation was, or what he might make out of it. But a guy like that, you don't share your troubles with him.

"Well," I said, "I knew she was *trying* to get it, but I didn't think she could. I guess it's like you say. You never know what you can do until you have to do."

"Mmm." He nodded, studying my face. "I was wondering. You know, any number of people called the store here for you; accounts who'd bought from sample pending your delivery. I explained the situation to them, about your shortage, and—"

"Swell," I said. "Why didn't you advertise it in the papers?"

"Now, Frank. I was only trying to help you. You can be very ingratiating, when you choose to, and I thought some of your clients might like to help you out in your hour of need."

I shook my head at him. The guy was off his goddamned rocker. "Sure, they would," I said. "This is Saks Fifth Avenue. I got a bunch of millionaire clients. I don't practically have to club 'em over the head to get a one-buck payment."

"Well," he smiled, sheepishly, "I suppose it was a rather forlorn hope. But . . . what I started to say was that I don't believe your wife was among those who called about you."

"So?" I said.

"Nothing," he said, hastily. "Naturally, you'd have called her from the jail. It just struck me as rather curious, your wife not calling and then sending the money in with another woman. I thought that, possibly—uh—"

I shrugged. It struck *him* as curious!

"I'll come clean with you," I said. "I didn't call my wife. I called all these scrubwomen and dishwashers I got for customers and I said they either laid it on the line, or I was through with them."

"Really, Frank!" He gave me a slap on the arm. "As a matter of fact, this woman—the girl—who brought the money in wasn't at all unattractive. Rather dowdy and weatherworn, but not bad withal."

"That must have been Frances Smith," I said. "The neighbor's girl. Joyce probably got herself a job, so she sent Frances with the money."

I lit a cigarette, casually, and dropped the match on the floor. That eager, foxy look went out of his eyes.

"Well, Frank. As long as you're here—"

"As long as I'm here," I said, "I'll take the dough I've got coming."

"Now, Frank," he pouted. "You mean you're angry with me? You're going to quit?"

"Well," I said. "I just supposed that—"

"Not at all. I'm sure you'll be extremely scrupulous from now on; just about have to, you know. You can go back to work right now, if you like."

I said I was pretty pooped; thought I'd better wait until Monday. He let me have twenty bucks against my pay, and I drove home.

The place smelled like a sewer. It stank with mildew and rotting food. I cleaned out the refrigerator, piling the stuff onto the junk on the table. Then, I just bundled it all up in the tablecloth, dishes and pans and everything, and threw the whole mess out into the garbage.

I opened all the windows, and hung the bedding on the line. There was still plenty to be done; there always would be in that place. But I let it go at that. I was feeling sort of limp, what with all the worry and nerve strain I'd been through. Almost too tired to wonder who had bailed me out or why she'd done it.

Maybe it would turn out to be a mistake after all.

It got dark. I put the windows back down, and drew the shades. I hadn't eaten much of anything while I was in jail; I couldn't eat that slop. So now I was pretty hungry. But there wasn't a damned thing in the cupboard but coffee and half a pint of whiskey. I took the whiskey in to the lounge and had myself a slug.

I leaned back, and put my feet up. I sipped and smoked, thinking about the way I'd been last night and how much better this was; thinking how a guy never knew when he was really well off, and maybe I hadn't done so bad for myself after all.

I began to relax. I started wondering again.

Now, who in the hell did I know ...

Who in the name of God could have ...

Someone was coming up the walk. Running, almost.

Up the walk and the steps and across the porch. I jumped up and threw the door open.

"Mona!" I said. "Mona, child. What is the—?"

She half fell into my arms. Sobbing, out of breath. I kicked the door shut and carried her over to the lounge.

"Baby," I said. "It's all right, baby. Old Dolly's got you, and—"

"Oh, Dolly, Dolly!" She rocked back and forth, hugging me. "I was s-so afraid, so afraid you might not be here and ... Don't let her get me, Dolly! Take me away! Help me to get away. I've got money, enough for both of us, Dolly! P-please, please, please—"

"Wait! Wait a minute!" I said, and I shook her by the shoulders. "Slow down, now. I'll do anything I can, honey, but I've got to know—"

"Take it, Dolly! You can have it all, but just take me with you."

She jabbed her hands into the pockets of her faded, old coat. She pulled them out again and money tumbled into my lap, crumpled wads of fives and tens and twenties.

"P-please, Dolly! Will you? Take the money and take me—"

"Sure," I said. "You bet I will. But we got to get a few things straight first. You took this money from your aunt?"

"Y-yes. This and the other, the money I gave to the man at the store. I d-didn't know what to think when you didn't come back. I knew something awful must have happened to you. You'd promised to come back, and I knew you wouldn't have broken your promise if you could help it. Anyone as g-good and nice as you were w-wouldn't—"

Her voice faltered. I patted her hand, uncomfortably.

"Yeah, sure," I said. "I just couldn't help it, see what I mean?"

"S-so I looked your number up in the phone book, and I called here. I called and called. And f-finally, today, I called the store, and the man said ... "

The rest of it came out with a rush:

Staples had given her the lowdown on me. She knew where the old woman kept her money. She'd tapped it for enough to get out, plus what she had here. Now, with what looked like five or six hundred dollars—and me just out from under one larceny rap—we were supposed to take off together. Live happily ever after, and so on.

And I wanted to—I wanted her; and I was grateful as hell. But, hell, how could I?

She was looking at me, pleading with her eyes. "D-don't you want to, Dolly? Was that why you said you were married—b-because you didn't really like me? I called and called here, and no one—"

"No, I wasn't lying to you," I said. "My wife left me. She doesn't figure in the deal any more, so that part's swell. But ... "

"She'll kill me when she finds out, Dolly! She'll know I took it, and—" She began to cry again, a low helpless sobbing that cut through me like a knife. "It's a-all right, Dolly. I d-don't mean to m-make you feel bad. I g-guess I should have known that you c-couldn't really l-like—"

"Baby," I said. "Listen to me, honey. Like isn't the word for the way I feel about you. I love you, understand? You've got to believe that. That's why we've got to go slow on this, because if we do it the wrong way—what you're suggesting—we'll never be together. They'll have us both in jail."

"But—"

"Listen to me. Let me ask the questions, and you answer 'em ... You're supposed to be out shopping tonight? Okay, the store was closed and you had to go on to another one. That takes care of that. Now, how about this dough your aunt had hidden. She doesn't know that you knew about it, does she?"

"N-no. But—"

"Just answer the questions. Where did she keep it? How did you happen to find out about it?"

"Down in the cellar. Behind some old boards and boxes. I was down there one day, cleaning out the furnace, and she didn't know I was there. She pulled the boards and boxes away, and there was a hole in the wall and the money was in it. In sort of a little suitcase. She took it out and counted it, mumbling and cursing—acting like she was half-crazy, a-and—she scared me to death, Dolly! I was afraid s-she might see me and—"

"Yeah, sure," I said. "The old miser act, huh? Did you ever see her down there again? When was the last time?"

"That was. It was the only time, about three months ago. The stairs are awfully steep, and I always go whenever there's anything to—"

"Uh-huh, sure. Well, don't you see, honey? It's all right. Anyway, it's all right for the present. Why, hell, it might be a year before she misses the dough."

She saw what I was leading up to, and she started getting frantic all over again. It might not be a year. Or even a day. The old gal might be checking over the dough right this moment, and—

"Stop it!" I said. "Get me, baby? I said to stop, and that's what I mean ... Your aunt doesn't know you took the money. She isn't going to know it. I go back on the job Monday. I'll have the three hundred-odd you got for me within a month or so. You'll put it back in that satchel, and you'll put this back tonight and—"

"*No!* I—"

"Yes! Don't you see, honey? We haven't got any choice. If you didn't go home tonight, the old gal would look for her dough right away. It's the first thing she'd think of. She'd know you'd taken it, and the police would pick you up in no time . . . You don't want that, do you? You see I'm right, don't you?"

"Y-yes." She nodded reluctantly. "Y-you—you really do love me, Dolly?"

"I wish I had time for a demonstration," I said, and I wasn't just woofing. "But you've been gone pretty long as it is. I'll drive you back over there, drop you off at the shopping center, and we'll get together in a day or two. Have a hell of a time for ourselves."

I stuffed the money back into her pockets, petting and kidding her until she was smiling. She was still pretty nervous and scared, but she thought she could swing it all right. She had the downstairs bedroom. The old woman slept upstairs, and once she went up for the night she stayed up.

"It's a cinch," I said. "You won't have a bit of trouble, baby. Now, let's have one big kiss and then we'll be on our way."

We had it. I headed the car across town. She rode with her head on my shoulder, hardly saying a word; pretty well at peace with the world. And that was the way I wanted her, of course, but me, I wasn't feeling so good.

Mona didn't know how often her aunt counted her money. She'd only caught her at it the one time, but there were probably plenty of other times she didn't know about. The old woman could be doing it right along, you know, when she sent Mona out to shop. It

figured that she would, a dame that liked dough as
well as she did. And if she did it before I got that
three-forty-five back ...

It wouldn't take her five minutes to beat the truth
out of Mona. Staples would have to return the money,
and I'd be returned to jail. On a double rap, probably:
the store's charges and a charge of getting Mona to
steal.

I wondered if maybe I wasn't playing this the wrong
way.

I couldn't think of any other.

Of course, if the old woman had had any real dough,
it would be different. If she'd had thousands instead of
hundreds—enough to do something with, you know,
enough so's you wouldn't mind sticking your neck
out—well, I'd have known exactly what to do, then.
She was a rotten, worthless old bitch. She had
something coming to her, and I was just the boy to
deliver it. And—and, hell! There didn't have to be
much risk. Some, sure, but not much. Because Pete
Hendrickson had something coming to him, too; and if
he wasn't built to be a fall guy I'd never seen one.

Yes, sir, I knew just how I'd use Pete. A plan popped
into my mind almost without me thinking. But for a
few hundred—huh-uh. Or even a few thousand.
When and if I ever pulled anything like that, I'd be
playing for the jackpot. One big haul, and then Mona
and—

Suddenly, I thought of something.

"Baby," I said. "Mona, honey. Does your aunt have
some other money around the house? I mean, if she
hardly ever digs into this cache in the basement—"

"Well," she hesitated, "I guess she must have; she
keeps it in her room, probably. I don't know because
the door's always locked, and she's never let me go in

there."

"Uh-hmm," I said. "She must have quite a bit, wouldn't you say? After all, she's got the day to day expenses of the two of you, and—"

"They're not very much, Dolly. We eat mostly rice and beans, and things that are cheap. I have to shop all around—buy stuff that the stores are about to throw out. We don't spend hardly anything."

"Yeah, but still ... "

"D-dolly ... " She drew closer to me. "I didn't w-want to tell you, but—I've had to do that—you know—a lot. I've had to do it for a long time. She's m-made me, and that's where ... "

. Jesus! It made me sick to think about it. Hustling this kid, making her hustle since she'd really been a kid ...

"Never you mind, honey," I said. "You won't have to do it any more, so you just don't think about it. I don't."

We were almost there, almost to the stores where I was supposed to let her out. She started getting the shakes again.

"Do I have to, Dolly? C-can't we just take the money, and—"

I shook my head. "No, baby, we can't. I mean, we really can't. We'd have to travel—we'd have to do plenty of traveling. We'd have to have money to live on. We just couldn't make it on this. It just ain't enough, know what I mean?"

"Well ... " She sat up on the seat, turned and looked at me eagerly. "I could get the rest, Dolly. There's a lot more, and I could get it, too."

"Huh! But you said—"

But she hadn't said that. I'd just assumed that she'd cleaned out all the old girl's cash. It was what I'd have done, if I'd been in a taking mood, and I supposed she had, too.

So there was more—a lot. But maybe there wasn't. What did a lot mean to a kid like this?

My hands were shaking on the wheel. I gripped it tighter, fighting to keep the excitement out of my voice.

"Now, let's just keep calm, baby," I said. "Old Dolly's in the saddle, and there's nothing to get up in the air about. N-now—now, how much is there? Tell papa, baby. What do you m-mean when you say a—"

"Well ... " She chewed her lip, frowning. "I'd have to count off for what I gave the man at the store, and this that I—"

"For God's sake!" I said. "Don't stop to do arithmetic problems! Spit it out! Just give it to me in round numbers."

She gave it to me.

My hands jerked on the wheel. I almost ran up on the curb.

"M-Mona," I said. "Baby, child. Sweet thing. Say that again."

"A hundred—will it be enough, Dolly? A hundred thousand dollars?"

I SAT AND stared at her, kind of stunned, and she looked at me, anxious eyed, her breasts rising and falling. We were like that for a minute or two, her staring at me hopefully and me too shocked-stupid to say anything. And then her face went dead again, and she said I'd better take her on home.

"It's all right, Dolly. I'm not afraid any more. She'll k-kill me, and then it'll all be over with and—"

"Hush your mouth, honey child," I said. "*She* isn't going to kill anyone. *She* isn't, get me?"

"But she will! She'll find out and—"

"Huh-uh. That ain't the way it's going to be, at all. Now, tell me something, baby. Where did an old bag like that get a hundred thousand dollars?"

"Well," she hesitated, "I'm not sure, but ... "

She couldn't remember much of anything about her early life. But the old lady had let drop a few things, and piecing it all together she had a pretty good idea about the source of that hundred grand. At least, it sounded good to me.

I started up the car again and drove on toward her place. Thinking. Wondering just how to put the proposition up to her. Or whether I really wanted to put it up to her.

"One more thing, honey. I think this is going to be all right—I mean, it could be all right. I think I can work it out so's you and I can go off together, and—and—" I couldn't get the words out: what I really wanted to say. I swallowed and made another try, coming in at it from an angle. "This Pete Hendrickson character; remember him, honey? Now, just suppose that Pete—"

She shivered and turned her head. You know. Sick, shamed, scared, just at the mention of Pete's name.

I gave her a little love pat, and called her a honey lamb.

"I'm sorry, baby. We won't talk about Pete any more, about any of those dirty bastards your aunt made you—well, never mind. What I was going to say was—was—suppose someone broke into your house and—"

"No," she said. "No, Dolly."

"But, baby. If—"

"No," she said again. "You're too nice. You've done too much. I couldn't let you do it."

I swallowed, feeling like I ought to be disappointed. Because this was the first crack I'd ever had at the big dough, and I figured it'd just about be the last. But I reckon that I was actually pretty relieved. I was glad that it wasn't going to happen.

"Well, all right," I said. "I just thought that—"

"She's got a gun. You might get hurt, or even killed," she said.

And I was back in business again.

We'd come to the shopping center where I was supposed to let her out. I pulled in at the curb, and stopped.

"The old gal's counting on me coming back to your house. Remember, honey? I told her I'd be back. So if I should drop around late some night and ... "

I laid it on the line for her. Not the whole stunt, because I didn't have it all figured out yet, but the main thing. What was going to have to happen to the old woman.

"You don't have to mix into it yourself, baby. All you have to do is have the dough ready for me to grab and call the cops after I've left."

"And then ... " The shine came back into her eyes, the deadness went out of her face. "And we could go away together, then, Dolly? We could be together after that?"

"In a week or so, sure. Just as soon as things cool off a little."

"Do it tonight, Dolly," she said. "Kill her tonight."

... Well, of course, doing it that night was out of the question. A deal like this, it was going to take some planning; there was Pete Hendrickson to be got ahold of and worked on. I told her we'd have to wait: probably I could swing it Monday. Meanwhile, she was to beat it on back to the house, and pretend like everything was hunky-dory.

"But what if she finds out I took that money, Dolly? If she finds out before Monday—"

"She won't," I said, making her believe it. Making myself believe it. "Beat it on home, now, and I'll talk to you again tomorrow night. I'll meet you right here around eight o'clock."

She hung back, scared as hell to face the old dame, just wanting to hang on to me. But I sweet-talked her, kind of getting hard-boiled at the same time, and finally she took off.

I watched her until she rounded the corner. Then, I made a u-turn in the street and headed for home.

Now that it was all settled—if, of course, I could

suck Pete in—I began to get cold feet. Or, maybe, I should say, I started to go cold on the deal. I wasn't really scared; hell, there wasn't anything to be scared about; and I sure wanted that little Mona and I sure wanted that hundred grand. But I just couldn't see myself doing what I'd have to do.

"Why, you're crazy, man!" I thought. "YOU'RE going to kill someone? YOU'RE going to kill a couple of people? Not you, fella. It just ain't in you."

I got about half way home, and then I jerked the wheel to the right and headed for town. I'd hardly eaten anything for the last three-four days. Maybe that was what was making me so shaky and nervous. Maybe things would look different to me with a good meal under my belt.

I toured around the business section for a few minutes, trying to think of something I wanted to eat and some decent place to eat in. I finally wound up at the same old joint I usually ate in—a little combination bar and grill around the corner from the store.

I sat down in a booth, and the waitress shoved a menu in front of me. There wasn't anything on it that sounded good, and anyway, one look at her and my stomach had turned flipflops. I don't know why it is, by God, but I can tell you how it is. Every goddamned restaurant I go to, it's always the same way . . . They'll have some old bag on the payroll—I figure they keep her locked up in the mop closet until they see me coming. And they'll doll her up in the dirtiest god-damned apron they can find and smear that crappy red polish all over her fingernails, and everything about her is smeary and sloppy and smelly. And she's the dame that always waits on me.

I'm not kidding, brother. It's that way wherever I go.

I told her to bring me a shot and a bottle of beer; I'd settle on something to eat later. But she was one of these salesmen, you know. She hung around, recommending "good things," the day's specials and so on; pointing 'em out with those goddamned red claws. So I put up with it just as long as I could, and then I gave her the old eye and told her off.

"Maybe you didn't hear me, sister," I said. "Maybe I better have the manager bring me that shot and the beer."

"B-but—" She looked like I'd hit her in the face, and it was just about as red as if I had. "I'm sorry, sir. I was j-just trying to—"

"And I'm trying to get a drink," I said. "Now, do I get it or not?"

I got it fast. But the next round I ordered, another girl brought it to me. Not that it made any difference, because she was just as bad as the first one; they all were; they always are. They may be okay up until then, but the minute I step in through the door of a place it's let's get sloppy, girls, here comes Dolly. The poor bastard ain't got enough trouble, so let's make him sick at his stomach.

I know how they do. They can't kid me a damned bit.

Well, anyway. I finished the first set-up and started on the second. I was sitting there sipping beer, thinking and trying not to think, when a shadow fell across the table.

"Ah, Frank"—Staples' lisping, oily voice. "So you are here, aren't you?"

I gave a little jump, and he grinned and sat down across from me. I asked him what he meant by that so-I-was-here stuff.

"A little bet I had with myself. I—Oh, thank you,

miss. A bowl of your delicious soup, if you please, and a tall glass of milk . . . As I was saying, Frank. I worked rather late at the store tonight, a special inventory, and afterwards I found myself in the mood for a pre-bedtime snack. But I do so hate to eat alone, you know; I'd almost rather do without. And just on the offchance that I might encounter some dear friend, I—Not you, of course. I had no idea that *you* would be eating out tonight . . . "

"This looks like I'm eating?" I said. "The wife had some girl friends in tonight so I got out of her way."

"How thoughtful of you. And how thoughtless of her; to entertain on your first night at home . . . Are you and the little woman getting along all right, Frank? You haven't quarreled?"

"Sorry to disappoint you," I said. "Now what's the pitch on this bet you made with yourself?"

"Oh, yes." He spooned soup into his pussy-cat mouth. "As I say, I was hoping to find someone to break bread with, and just on the offchance that you or one of the boys might be here, I glanced through the window . . . "

He grinned, waiting for me to feed him the straight line. I let him wait, taking another slug of beer, and his lips pulled down in a little pout.

"I couldn't see you from the street, Frank. And yet I knew you were here. Aren't you interested in knowing how?"

I was curious about it. But I shrugged and said it made me no difference.

His eyes glinted spitefully. "The atmosphere of the place, Frank. The look on the faces of those poor girls. Tell me, if you don't like the food and the service here why don't you go some place else?"

"What's the use?" I said. "They're all alike."

"Oh? But—" He studied me puzzledly; then, his head moved in a nod, and he smiled in a way I didn't understand. "Yes," he said, "yes, I suppose they are all alike if ... "

"Yeah?"

"Nothing. This is quite cozy, Frank; it's always such a joy to talk to you ... I trust you're fully readjusted after your recent ordeal? You harbor no ill-will toward me?"

"A swell guy like you?" I said. "How could I?"

"I'm so glad. Incidentally, inasmuch as we are such good friends ... "

"Fire away."

"How in the name of heaven did you get so deeply in the hole? After all, the other collectors also had the rain to contend with, and they didn't appropriate more than three hundred dollars in company funds."

"Well," I said. "Well, you see, Staples ... "

"Yes, Frank?"

I couldn't tell him. I wouldn't have told him even if I could have found the right words, because it just wouldn't have been smart. But I couldn't find the right words.

"Are you fed up, Frank? Is that it? Feel like your best effort gains you no more than your worst, that existence itself has become pointless?"

Well, like I say, I couldn't tell him; but he hadn't missed it very far. I couldn't get out and hit the old ball any more because I just didn't give a damn any more. And I guess there's nothing that can make a guy give a damn if he doesn't feel like it.

"How about it, Frank?" His lisp was gone. "You may as well tell me now, if that's the case."

"Hell," I said. "You talk like a man in a paper hat. What's the difference anyway?"

He didn't bother to answer me. Just waited. The difference was that if I couldn't earn my dough, I'd probably go back to stealing it. And I might skip out with a wad before he could nail me.

"I don't get you," I said, stalling for time. "If you were worried, why didn't you jump me about it this afternoon instead of—"

"I'm not the jumping kind, Frank. I always think things through, put all the various pieces together, before I act. Now, what happened to that money?"

A month or so later on I could have told him to go to hell; that, sure I was fed up with the damned stinking job and who wouldn't be, and so what the hell about it? But it wasn't a month or so later, and until it was—until everything had cooled off and it was safe to skip with Mona—I had to have a reason for staying in this crummy burg. I had to hang onto the job.

" ... you understand, dear boy." He was quizzing me again. "I'm not merely being nosy. If it's simply something shady or unwise, if, for example, you spent it on a woman or took a little flyer on the ponies ... "

I looked up, meeting his eyes at last. He'd rung the bell with that last bit. He'd shown me how to get off the hook, and he'd also opened the way for me to ask him some questions.

"You remember that sales letter I showed you a while back? From that oil company down in Oklahoma?"

"Letter?" He shrugged. "I think you've showed me at least a dozen. For a man with some pretensions to sophistication, you seem to have landed on a truly amazing number of sucker lists. But—" He broke off, staring at me. "Oh, *no!*" he said. "No, Frank! You didn't send *that* outfit any money."

"Yeah," I looked sheepish. "I guess I did, Stape."

"But I distinctly told you—"

"Yeah, I know," I said, "but look at all the other things you told me. About the chances you missed when you were running a store down there years ago, and—"

"But my dear Frank! That was entirely different. I had a chance to buy land—leases. The real thing, not merely wild promises on paper."

"Well, I'll know better next time," I said. "You could have got in on the ground floor, huh, Stape?"

It was his favorite topic, the one thing he'd really talk to you about instead of jabbing you with the needle. Once you got him on the subject of oil and this town where he'd managed his first store, he was a different guy entirely.

"... you never saw anything like it, Frank. Nominally, it was the sorriest land in the world. Rocky, eroded, worn out. Then, the boom came and these poor farmers—people who actually hadn't had enough to eat a few months before—were suddenly rich beyond their wildest dreams. Why, I personally know of one little eighty-acre plot that went for a million and a half dollars, and—"

I whistled, wonderingly, cutting in on him; sliding in one of the questions I wanted to ask. "I don't suppose they all cashed in that heavy though, did they? I mean, some of 'em probably sold out too early or—"

"That's right. That's right, Frank. It just seemed too good to be true, you know. In a great many instances, the first lease hound that came along and shook forty or fifty or a hundred grand under a farmer's nose—"

"Cash?" I whistled again. "You mean they actually swung that much *cash* at 'em?"

"Oh, yes, and even much larger sums. The psychological effect, you know; and then these people were poorly educated and inclined to be suspicious of banks. Cash they understood. A check—well, that to them was nothing more than a piece of paper."

"What about the people like that, anyway?" I said. "I'll bet a lot of them didn't know what the hell to do with the money after they got it."

"True. Oh, so true, Frank. You or I, now—if I were ever able to get my hands on any substantial sum . . ." He broke off, sighing, and dipped into the soup again. "Yes, Frank. It was an experience that might have permanently embittered a man of a less philosophical turn of mind. Here was poor little me, filled with appreciation for the finer things in life yet lacking the money to achieve them. And here were these loutish creatures with scads of money and no appreciation whatsoever. Why, in case after case, they wouldn't even buy themselves the necessities of life. They simply went on living as they always had, and hoarded their tens of thousands."

I grinned. "I'll bet that really did burn you, Stape. You right in the middle of all that cabbage, and not being able to latch onto it."

"Oh, I tried, Frank," he nodded, seriously. "I tried, oh, so terribly hard. But I'm afraid I was a little green and callow in those days. A trifle clumsy. The only result of my efforts was a sudden transfer to another store."

I had another round of drinks while he was finishing his snack. Then he left for his hotel, and I started for home. I still hadn't eaten anything, but I was feeling pretty good. The talk with Staples had warmed me back up on the deal.

No, I didn't really know anything. All I had to go on

was the few things that Mona remembered, or thought she remembered, and the little that she'd picked up from the old woman's remarks. But all in all, and taken with what Staples had told me, it seemed to add up.

They'd lived down south at one time—Mona and the old woman and some other people she couldn't remember: her own folks, I figured. It must have been the south or southwest, because it was warmer and things stayed green longer—*she remembered, or thought she did*. And there'd been towers—oilfield derricks—and ... And that was about all, as much as she could tell me. Why they'd come up here to settle down, I didn't know; so there was kind of a hole in the picture there. But I didn't see that it was too important, and the rest was solid enough.

Oil had been struck on their farm down south. The old woman had sold out for a hundred grand. Or maybe she'd got even more, and was just hoarding the hundred grand. Low down white trash. Too miserly to let go of a buck, and not knowing what the hell to buy with it if she did let go. Sitting on a hundred thousand, and hustling her own niece for bean money.

Yeah, it figured.

I wanted it to be that way, so that's the way it was.

I PICKED up a few groceries the next morning, and had a real meal for a change. French toast with bacon, hashed brown potatoes, fruit cocktail and coffee. I ate and ate, grinning to myself, thinking by God they might *think* they could starve old Dolly to death but they had another goddamned think coming. To hell with those damned sloppy waitresses. To hell with that damned bitchy Joyce, and Doris, and Ellen and . . . and all those other tramps. Old Dolly could take care of himself until he got someone decent to do the job. And, brother, that happy hour was not far away.

I refilled my coffee cup, and lighted a cigarette. I sat back in my chair, relaxing. Pete Hendrickson was the next step. I'd look him up today on the quiet— naturally it wouldn't do to be seen with him—and . . .

I choked, and banged down my cup.

Pete.

I didn't know where the guy lived.

The last address I'd had on him was the one he'd skipped from, you know, before he went to work at that greenhouse. And where the hell he might be living now, God only knew. He might not even have an address since he lost his job. He could be bunking in a boxcar somewhere or sleeping under a culvert.

I jumped up cursing, paced back and forth across the living room. I thought, *by God, I might have known it! I knock my brains out to shape up a sweet deal and someone screws it up for me!*

I don't know how long I paced around, cursing and ranting, before I finally got a grip on myself. Then, I got out the phone book, looked up the number of the greenhouse and dialed it.

I got the foreman on the wire.

I said, "Please, sor, iss Olaf Hendrickson speaking. Iss very important dot I speak to my brudder, Pete."

"Not here any more," he said. "Sorry."

"Perhaps you vould tell me vere—"

"Nope, nope," he said, curtly, before I could ask him the question. "Don't give out information like that. Not sure, anyway."

"Please, sor," I said. "Iss—"

"Sorry." He banged up the receiver.

Well, I'm a funny guy, though. People try to screw me up, to keep me from doing what I got to do, I go at it all the harder.

I looked at the clock. I shaved and brushed my teeth, and gandered the clock again. Eleven-fifteen. Just about right. I got in my car, and headed for the other side of town.

It was pretty close to noon when I got to this beer parlor, the one just down the street from the greenhouse. I picked up the name and address as I drove by, and stopped at a drugstore in the next block. I waited in my car until the noon whistles blew. Then, I got out and stood looking down the street.

My hunch had been right. Workmen were coming out of the greenhouse and making a beeline for the beer parlor. I gave them a few minutes to get inside and get settled. I went into the drugstore, then, and called the place from a booth telephone.

The phone rang and rang. Finally, someone snatched it off the hook, the proprietor or a bartender or maybe even a customer, and hollered hello.

"There's a fellow there named Pete Hendrickson," I said. "One of the boys from the greenhouse. Will you call him to the phone, please?"

He didn't answer me; just turned away from the phone and shouted, "Pete—Pete Hendrickson! Any of you guys named Hendrickson?"

Someone shouted something back, and someone else laughed; and this guy spoke into the phone again. "He ain't here, mister. Ain't at the greenhouse no longer, either."

"Gosh," I said. "I've just got to talk to him. I wonder if there's anyone around who could tell me where—"

"Hang on," he said, pretty short, like I was giving him a hard time. "ANY OF YOU GUYS KNOW WHERE ... "

They didn't. Or if they did, they weren't saying.

"Sorry, mister," this guy said. "Any other little thing I can do for you?"

I told him yeah. "Go take a flying jump at yourself, you snotty bastard." And I slammed up as he started to cuss.

Well, that had been my best bet but it wasn't my only one. Characters like Pete Hendrickson were my meat. I knew just what they'd do, just where they'd go. Sure, it'd taken me weeks to run him down before; and I could work out in the open then instead of slipping around like I had to now. But that had been different. I hadn't been looking for him for myself. This time it was for me—for me and Mona and a hundred grand—and by God I'd find him.

I drove into town, and parked at the foot of skid row.

I got out and started walking.

I must have walked fifteen miles that afternoon. Past the employment agencies with the bums hanging around in the front. Past the flop houses with their fly-specked windows and stinking lobbies. Past the greasy spoons. Past the pool halls and wine joints and cheap beer parlors.

Hell, it was Saturday afternoon wasn't it? And even if he had a home, a guy like Pete wouldn't stay in on Saturday afternoon. He'd be down here where he could stretch a few dimes into a party. Where he could guzzle and scoff and have enough left over for a flop.

So I walked and walked, just strolling from place to place, going around and around and around. And Saturday afternoon went away, and it was Saturday night.

I was too jumpy to eat—not that I could have got anything to eat, anyhow. I found a bar that wasn't too completely crummy looking, and threw down a few double shots. Then I started walking again.

He had to be here, someplace. Son-of-a-bitch, he just *had* to! If he wasn't around here, then he must have left town and—

I gritted my teeth together. *No! NO! He couldn't do that to me. They couldn't do that to me.*

Saturday night.

Eight o'clock Saturday night. Still no Pete . . . and it was almost time to meet Mona.

I bought a pint of whiz, and went back to my car. I yanked the cap with my teeth, making them ache to beat hell and liking the ache. I threw down a slug—two or three slugs. I dropped the jug down on the seat, and stepped on the starter.

High? Man, I was higher than a kite; but not from the old gravy. It was the kind of high you get on when

you got to do something and can't. When you've got to
have the answers and you don't know any.

What was I going to do now? What was I going to tell
Mona? I'd told her I was going to fix it, and I'd reached
the point where I could almost feel that hundred
grand ...

I fingered the cap off the bottle and took another
long drink ... Tell her? Tell her nothing. If I could dig
up Pete tomorrow or the next day, fine. If not—and I'd
better not hang around town much longer after that—
well, she'd have a few days of hope before she found
out the truth. And me, I wouldn't have had anything
more than I was entitled to.

It was the only thing to do, as I saw it. Brush her off
on the questions. Play it close to the vest. Make her
happy and grateful, and then—You know. Nothing
wrong with that, was there? I wasn't taking anything
that she wasn't perfectly willing to give me.

"Nothing wrong," I said—and I said it out loud.
"Dolly Dillon says there's nothing wrong with it—the
rotten son-of-a-bitch!"

So, anyway, I admitted it; and I was mad enough at
myself to bite nails. But I knew I was going to go right
ahead, just the same.

She was waiting in the shadows of a tree a few
doors down from the super-market. She climbed into
the car, laying a little sack of groceries up behind the
seat, and I stepped on the gas. The jerk threw her
against me. She moved away, looking a little fright-
ened, her voice trembling.

"W-where are we going, Dolly? I've been away from
the house quite a while, and—"

"I won't keep you long," I said. "What's the matter?
You act like you're not glad to see me."

"Oh, no, Dolly! I mean, I am glad. But—Is everything

67

all right? W-we ... you're still going to do it?"

"Didn't I say so?" I said.

"Monday? N-no later than Monday, Dolly? I'm scared to death she'll—"

"I told you, didn't I?" I said. "You want me to put it in writing?"

I drove across a railroad spur, turned down a dirt road and parked. There weren't any streetlights over that way, and there wasn't any traffic. I put my arms around her, and pulled her against me.

I kissed her, and ran a hand over her. And what happened then was so wild and wonderful that—well, I don't know how to say it. I guess a hop-eater's dream might be something like that.

I've been around, see? I'm not one of these old country boys that can work up a boil around a lingerie counter. I've known the twenty-dollar gals and the nicey-nice babes who were just out for kicks. But I'd never known anything like that before.

Then, it was all over—it was, as far as I was concerned. But that didn't seem to mean nothing to her. I said, "Baby ... " and then I said, "My God, honey ... " and finally I said, "What the hell is this?"

I shoved her away, and got back on my own side of the seat. That seemed to break the spell, as they say in story books.

"I'm s-sorry." She bit her lip, trying not to look at me, looking ashamed. "I j-just love you so much that—that—"

But how about a babe like this? Maybe I had the wrong angle on things. Maybe the old woman was just selling something to keep it from going for free.

That thought went in and out of my mind fast. It didn't even have time to say hello before I'd booted it out in the cold and slammed the door. Because even a

68

damned fool could see that this kid was a doll, just as sweet and innocent as they come. And naturally with everything I was doing for her—with everything she *thought* I was doing for her—she wanted to do something special for me.

That was the way I wanted it, the way it should be. After all the tramps I'd been tied up with, it was about time I met someone who was grateful and loving and appreciative.

I told her she was swell, and everything was swell. I just hadn't wanted to hold her up tonight when she was already late. "About this gun your aunt has," I said, starting the car. "Where does she keep it?"

"Upstairs. In her room . . . Dolly—"

"She keeps the key to the room with her? Swell. Now you get your clothes straightened out, and I'll drive you back to the shopping center."

"Dolly"—she started brushing at her clothes—"What—how are you going to do it, Dolly? I mean, I ought to know if—"

"Huh-uh," I said. "You don't need to know a thing. If you had it on your mind you might accidentally give it away, so just forget about it."

"B-but—"

"You hear? Forget it," I said. "All you have to do is be at home Monday night between eight-thirty and nine."

"Eight-thirty or nine?"

"Or ten. Somewhere along there," I said.

"You asked—you started to ask about Pete Hendrickson last night. What does he—?"

"Nothing," I said, and it didn't look like I was lying about that. Pete wasn't going to have anything to do with it. I wasn't going to. And I sure felt sorry for her, but what could I do? "Now leave it lay, will you?" I said. "You keep asking questions I'm liable to think you don't trust me."

"I'm sorry. I just wondered what—"

"Here's where you get out," I said, and I handed her the groceries. "Now, hurry on home and don't worry about a thing. Everything's going to be fine."

She opened the door of the car and started to get out. She turned back around worriedly, apologetically, her lips parted for another try.

I leaned forward and kissed her, gave her a little punch. "Beat it," I said. "You hear me, honey? I want to see you move."

She smiled. She beat it. I drove away.

I made a few more tours of skid row, and it was still no soap. It looked like Pete must have jumped town. I got a bite to eat and bought another pint, and drove home, figuring, well, hell, maybe that's the way it's supposed to be.

I think I told you earlier that this shack of ours was on a railroad siding, that there was the tracks on one side and a wrecking yard on the other? Anyway, I meant to tell you. So I drove home that night, and there was a string of cars shuttled onto the siding: an empty box and a gondola and a couple of flats. And I thought, oh, oh, no damned sleep in the morning. They'll be in here humping those cars at six a.m.; and—

I gulped. I stood staring at the open door of the box car, and I sort of froze in my tracks.

It was dark on that street. Ours was the only house in the block. I'd already locked up the car and I knew I'd never have time to get my hands on a wrench or something to slug with before this guy could get to me. Because he'd already started toward me. He'd swung down out of the door of the box, a hell of a big guy, and was coming across the yard. And I couldn't see what he looked like, of course. But I reckoned he wasn't up to any good or he wouldn't have been ...

He stopped about six steps away from me.

"Dillon?" he said. "Iss Dillon, yess?"

And I sagged back against the car.

"P-Pete," I said weakly. "Pete Hendrickson."

10

HE'D TAKEN the five I gave him the night before and jungled up with some 'boes down on Salt Creek. They'd all got on a hell of a wine binge and he hadn't woke up until tonight, needing a drink like a baby needs its mother. A drink and some chow and an inside flop. And there was just one guy he could think of who might hold still for a bite. I had been "so nice" to him. The "fife dollars" I had given him, and I had spoken of a "chob," so . . .

He cleared his throat, uncomfortably, misunderstanding my silence. "I did not go to your door, Dillon. Your vife—you have a vife, yess?—I was afraid of alarming; so late at night to see a bum like me at the door. So I vait in the box until I hear your car, and—"

His voice trailed away.

I snapped out of the jolt he'd given me.

"I'm glad you came by," I said. "I've been wanting to see you. Come on inside and—"

"Better I had not. Such a bum I look, and your vife vould not like. If you could chust—vell, a dollar or two—chust until I find vork . . ."

"Huh-uh," I said, and took him by the arm. "You need a lot more than that, Pete. Come on in, and I'll tell you about it, and, no, don't worry about the wife.

She's away on a little trip."

I got him inside. I saw that the shades were drawn, and I turned on the light, and gave him the opened pint.

He killed it at a gulp, shuddered, sighed. I passed him the fresh pint and gave him a cigarette.

He took another drink, drew a long drag on the cigarette. He leaned back in his chair, sighing.

"Ahhhhh," he said, just like that. "Ahhhhh. My life you have safed, Dillon."

"Maybe not your life," I said. "Just about forty years of it. I think that's the stretch in this state for raping a minor."

It didn't register on him for a moment. He'd been stuck in the basement, and now he was riding the express car up; and it wasn't stopping for signals.

He took another swig from the jug. He wiped his mouth, and said I was a nice man. He said I was a "chentleman" and a fine friend. And then he said, *"Vot!* Rape?" And leaned forward in his chair.

"You heard me," I said. "Old lady Farrell's niece. Mona."

"B-b-but," he said. "B-b-but—"

"Yeah?"

"A lie it iss! I—I—" He swallowed and his eyes shifted away from mine. "With the girl I was, yess. Vy not? I vork, and dot is some of my pay. She does not object, it iss agreeable with her and—"

"It was, huh?" I said. "Maybe she took it away from you, huh?"

And I thought, oh, you dirty bastard! You dirty lying bastard! You just wait.

"Vell"—he started to smirk, then straightened his face when he saw the look I was giving him. "Vell, no. I haf told you how it vas. I vork, she iss the pay."

"And she's a minor. A child in the eyes of the law."

"But she iss not! She could not be! And anyway, I did not force—"

"The old woman says she's a minor," I said. "She says you threatened to kill her and the girl, and then you took it."

"B-but—but—"

He lifted the bottle again. He stared at me, his eyes crafty.

"I t'ink maybe you—maybe you not tell truth, Dillon."

"All right," I said.

"Vy—vy vould she do such a thing? I am not the first; many others there have been. And—and how you know, anyvay?"

"Let it go," I said. "I felt like I'd given you kind of a raw deal getting you fired, and I wanted to make up for it. But as long as you think I'm lying, let it go."

I stood up and took out my wallet. I got out a couple of ones, letting him see them, and then I shoved them back and took out a five. I held it out to him.

"And take the bottle along with you, too," I said. "You'd better have a good one before they pick you up."

"B-but—" He drew back from the money. "I did not mean to offend. It iss chust—"

"Just for your own satisfaction," I said, "why don't you call the old gal up? There's the phone. Ask her if she isn't going to send you over the road just as soon as she can arrange it."

"B-but if I did dot—"

"But it isn't true, remember? I'm lying to you."

His face was turning gray. He took such a slug out of the pint that he almost killed it.

"Dillon," he said. "How—vot—vot *iss?*"

I sat down in front of him. I looked him in the eye and began to talk.

So maybe he wasn't the first one with Mona, I said. But could he prove it? And could he prove that she wasn't a minor, and that she and the old woman had agreed to the deal? It would be his word against theirs. And *he* had a police record and a bad rep for drinking.

Why was the old gal doing this to him? Well, she was a pure mean bitch and low down as all hell (*he nodded*), and she was sore at him, remember? They'd had a knock-down dragout brawl before he'd quit working for her (*he nodded again*), and she was plenty burned up about it. She was out for blood, that baby, and she meant to stick him.

Pete shook his head dully. A thin thread of slobber oozed down from the corner of his mouth, and he brushed it away.

"Vy?" he said. "I do not doubt you, Dillon, but vy does she tell—"

"Because she thought I was on her side, see?" I lied. "I went there trying to trace you down for the store, and you know it was just business with me; I wasn't sore at you at all, and I proved it to you. But, anyway, she figures I am, and I play along with her, so just as I'm leaving, she says to come back and let her know if you're still there at the greenhouse. She's got an idea how we can make it plenty tough on you.

"Well, like I say, I wasn't sore at you at all. I'm really your good friend and I proved it, didn't I? (*He hesitated, nodded firmly.*) So I go back and tell her you've quit the greenhouse, and then I ask her what the score is. I want to find out, see, so I can tip you off.

"I guess maybe she got a little suspicious of me about then because all she'll say is never mind; the cops will be able to find you and when they do it'll be just too bad. But I kept on hanging around, pretending like I'm burned up with you, too, and anxious to help her, and finally she tells me what she has in mind..."

I coughed and turned my head. Man, it was all I could do to keep from busting out laughing! ... That slobber running down his chin again; and his eyes— glazed and bugged out like marbles. He was one scared bastard, and I'm crapping you negative.

"Well, I was afraid to try to talk her out of it," I went on. "She'd have seen I was really your friend, see, and she'd probably have called the cops right away. So I said swell, I was all for it, but maybe she wouldn't be able to make it stick. Maybe it would be better if I looked you up and brought you there. You know; had a few drinks with you and then suggested that we go over there for a party. We'd frame you—I told her—see? We'd call the cops in, and ..."

Yeah, it was pretty wild, but he was a pretty dumb guy. Didn't have much education, anyway. And I guess he'd been pushed around plenty by the cops. He stared at me, his lips too stiff to move, his face turning green under the gray. And I coughed and turned my head again.

"V-vot ... I haf some time, Dillon? I can get out of town before—"

"How far would you get?" I said. "The cops have your mug and prints. They put out a flier on you, and they pick you up in no time."

"B-but vot—"

"I'm telling you," I said. "She gave me until Monday night, so Monday night we go over there. I'll go in first and tell her you'll be along in a few minutes, and then you slip up on the porch and I start talking to her. I tell her I'm sticking my neck out a mile, so how about a roll with the gal for my trouble. And she'll go for it, see; she practically propositioned me already. So then I say I've got to be sure she won't try to stick me some time. She'll have to give me something in writing to show that she and the gal consented to the deal. That the kid's over twenty-one and she's done it before and—Well, what's the matter?"

He'd been frowning a little. I gave him a hard look, and he cleared his throat apologetically.

"It . . . a little strange, it sounds. You t'ink she vould do such?"

"Sure, she will. It's a cinch."

"Den vy iss it necessary for me to be dere?"

"Why?" I said. And for a minute I couldn't think of anything else to say. "Why, dammit, I don't need to explain that to you, do I?"

"If you vould not mind, pleass. So mixed up I am, I cannot—"

"Why, it's because she's liable to hang back, know what I mean? She's liable to think I'm trying to pull a fast one on her. So I step to the door and say, well, here you are now. I want that statement. I want it right then or the deal don't go no further. I'll tip you off and tell the cops it's a frame, and she'll be in heap big trouble."

He nodded, his face clearing. He hesitated.

"Vould you—You do not t'ink perhaps you could go to the police now and—?"

"I thought of that," I said, "but I'm afraid it wouldn't work. They'd probably lock you up while they were trying to get to the bottom of things; and maybe they wouldn't stick you on a rape rap but you'd still be in for a long jolt. It's a pretty messy deal, you know, anyway you look at it. Even if it wasn't rape—"

"It vas not! I svear it, Dillon!"

"—it still looks bad. You can't make it look any

other way. There are at least a couple of charges they could stick you on, and they'd damned well give you the maximum on each."

He sighed; nodded again.

"You are right, my good friend. So, if you are villing to do me dis great favor ... "

"I owe it to you," I said. "I got you fired, and now I'm trying to square things. Anyway, it's a pleasure to put a crimp in that old bitch's tail."

He told me I was a nice man and a "chentleman," again. He looked at the bottle, set it down on the end table, and stood up. "So much you haf done, I am ashamed to ask—"

"Sit down," I said. "You're going to stay here. Stay right here until this is all over with."

"B-but"—he sat down again; he didn't need any urging at all—"It iss too much."

"Nuts," I said. "I'm glad to have some company. Now how about some bacon and eggs?"

His eyes filled up; I thought, by God, he was going to start blubbering. "My good friend," he said. "My fine friend." And he brushed his nose on his sleeve.

"There's just one thing," I said. "You'll have to stay under cover, understand? Keep inside the house and don't let anyone know you're around here. It wouldn't look good, know what I mean, if the old gal decided to get tough and we had to go to the police. They'd figure that we were buddies, see? Get the idea that one of us was lying and the other was swearing to it."

"So," he said. "I vill do as you say."

I fixed him some grub.

I went out and got more whiskey.

I made him go to bed in the bedroom, and I took the lounge.

I fell asleep fast, but along about three in the

morning I woke up, feeling kind of cramped and like something was hugging me.

Something was. The bedclothes. I was all tucked in like a two-year-old.

I started to lug the stuff back in to him; and then I remembered Mona, that sweet child, and the way he'd taken advantage of her. So I just took what blankets I wanted, and dropped the rest on the floor.

Let the son-of-a-bitch freeze. He'd be plenty hot in the place he was going to.

11

THE NEXT DAY was Sunday, and it was just about the damnedest longest day I ever spent in my life.

Pete was pretty well leveled off of his binge. His mind was about as clear as it ever got to be, and he was over his first scare. So he starts to worrying, wondering, firing the questions at me. And frankly my mind wasn't very clear. Everything was kind of mashed together inside, like I'd been crawling through a rat hole.

I started feeding him whiskey right away. I got out my collection cards and pretended like I was working. But I couldn't hedge him off. They kept coming, the "vys" and the "vots" and the "hows" until, man, I was almost ready to murder him right there.

"I told you" (I told him). "Goddammit, Pete, how many times do I have to explain it? I get this business in writing from her, and then she's screwed. You could whip her with a wet rope and she wouldn't dare let out a peep."

"But"—he kept shaking his head—"but so strange, it seems. Like a movie almost. It iss hard to believe that she vill—"

"Well, she will! Wait and see if she doesn't."

"Still"—he kept on shaking his goddamned head—

"it iss hard to ... it iss so strange. For her to be so angry with me over somet'ing dat—For her to tell you of her plans, and for you to—"

"All right," I said. "I'm lying. I made it all up. Why the hell would I lie to you, for Christ's sake?"

"Pleass! My good friend, my dear friend. I did not mean—"

"What do you mean?"

"Vel. I vas chust wondering. I merely wished to ask vy ..."

No, I don't think he was actually suspicious; he was too well sold on me and him being swell friends. It was more as though he was afraid I was going off half-cocked: like maybe the old woman had been tossing some bull and I'd got the wind up over nothing. Or maybe I was setting a bear trap to catch a skunk: making such a big deal out of it that we were liable to get screwed up in the machinery.

Anyway, he kept on and on, fussing and quizzing and worrying out loud, until by God! I had just all I could take and I couldn't take any more. It was about an hour or so after dinner when it happened. I'd gone out to the delicatessen and bought enough damned grub to feed a horse, thinking, you know, that a good scoff would keep him quiet for a while. But all through the meal he was making with the talk—talking with his goddamned big mouth full—and afterwards he had to help with the dishes; I mean he insisted on it. And the talk kept on, on and on and on until ...

The words began to dance through my mind. *Vy, vot, vy-vot*—faster and faster and yet somehow slow—*vy-vot, VY-VOT. VYVOTVY VYVOT ... Why, what, why-what, whywhat. Why? WHY? WHY? ...*

All of a sudden something seemed to snap inside of my head. It was just like I *wasn't* any more, like I'd just shriveled up and disappeared. And in my place there was nothing but a deep hole, a deep black hole, with a light shining down from the top.

The light began to move downward. It rushed downward with a swishing, screaming sound. It reached the bottom of the pit, and shot back upward again. And then I came back from wherever I had been; and Pete and I were standing in the front room. And I was talking to him.

Very quietly.

"You're right," I said. "The whole thing's a damned lie. She isn't out to get you; I'm out to get her. She's got a pile of dough, see, a hundred thousand dollars, and no one else knows about it. I figured on bumping her off and grabbing it, and making it look like you—"

"Please"—he patted my shoulder awkwardly. "Ogscuse, my good friend. I am vorried and I talk too much, but now I vill say no more."

"I'm telling you," I said. "I'm laying it on the line for you. Now get the hell on out of here, and forget the whole deal."

He put both hands on my shoulders and pushed me down into a chair. He gave me another little pat, looking sad and apologetic. "Soch a bum, I am. So much you do for me, and not'ing I do but chatter like a skvirell. Vell! No more. Now you vill rest, and the dishes I vill finish."

"I don't want you to," I said. "All I want you to do is—"

"And I vill not do it," he said firmly. "Only the dishes I vill do, and keep my so-big mouth shut."

Well I'd told him. And even if I'd been able to go on telling him—and I couldn't—he wouldn't have listened. He finished the dishes. He mopped up the kitchen, and scrubbed the oil cloth on the table. He came back into the living room, and he poured a very small drink for himself and a big one for me.

He kept his word. There were no more questions. But I could see he was busting with them, that he was itching inside like he'd swallowed a poison ivy bush. And seeing him that way, it was ten times worse than if he'd actually talked.

I poured him a big drink. I made him take three or four big slugs, but it didn't seem to help much. I tried to get his mind off of what he was thinking about— what I was thinking about.

I got out a deck of cards and a box of matches, for chips, and we played a few hands of draw. We switched from poker to cooncan, and then on to monte and faro, and then on to a lot of wild games like baseball and spit-in-the-ocean.

The cards seemed to help some. They were a long time in doing it, but finally they did. He began to hum, to kind of mumble-sing. The first thing I knew I was doing it with him. We grinned and came in on the chorus together; it was *Pie in the Sky,* as I recollect. And by the time we got to the end we'd dropped the cards, and were laughing like fools.

"Dillon"—he wiped his eyes—"soch a pleasure. Good friends, good viskey, a good song. I do not belieff I haf heard that song since—"

"I'll bet I can tell you," I said. "Up in the northwest, wasn't it? Were you ever up around Washington and Oregon?"

"Vas I! Vy in 1945—"

"Nineteen forty-five!" I said. "Why, hell, I was there myself that year. Running a pots and pans crew ..."

Well, I guess it wasn't so strange, because guys like us would just naturally get around a lot; we wouldn't do the same kind of work but we'd land in a lot of the same places. It seemed funny, though; strange, I mean. And when I could make myself forget—the other—it seemed kind of good.

We sang one song after another. Keeping our voices down, of course. We sang and drank and talked, and I guess we got pretty tight before the evening was over. I guess I got even tighter than he did. The day had been endless, you know; it had taken everything I had out of me. So now I filled up on the music and the talk and the drink, and I got tight as a fiddle.

"What's it all about, Pete?" I said. "What the hell are we looking for, anyway?"

"Looking, Dillon?"

"Yeah. Chasing from one place to another, when we know they're all alike. Moving from job to job, when we know they're all alike. That there isn't a goddamned one of 'em that doesn't stink."

"Vell"—he scratched his head. "I do not t'ink ve are looking, Dillon. I t'ink radder ve are trying not to look."

"Yeah?"

"Yess. At somet'ing ve alvays find whereffer ve go . . . No, no more. And no more for you, my friend. Vork you must do tomorrow, so now you shall haf coffee."

"Don't want any coffee," I said. "Want another drink. Wanta talk. Wanta—"

"Coffee," he said, firmly, getting up. "And then bed."

He went out into the kitchen. I heard the water tap go on, and then there was a lot of sloshing. Sloshing and sloshing and sloshing. I listened to it. My head began to ache again, and all the good feeling went out of me.

I got up and staggered to the kitchen door. I stood

staring at him, and the blood pounded through my brain.

"Why?" I said. "What the hell kind of slop-gut are you?"

"Vot?" He whirled around startled. "I do not under—"

"Why didn't you do it in the first place?" I said. "You knew it had to be done. Everything was swell and you had to screw it up. Why? An-answer me, you dirty son-of-a-bitch! Why ... w-why didn't you wash out that coffee pot ... ?"

I began to bawl.

I started to slide down the door jamb, and he picked me up in his arms and carried me into the bedroom ...

... That Monday, the next day, was a toughie. I wasn't bothered about him any more, except for worrying that he might show himself outside the house, because after the way he'd acted he had it coming to him. But there were plenty of other things on my mind. I couldn't concentrate on my work, and this was one day I had to concentrate. Staples had his eye on me. If I sloughed off very much I'd be out of a job, and that job I had to have. For a while.

So I had the job to think about, to make a good showing on. And I had all this other stuff, the hundred grand and Mona, and what I was going to have to do to get 'em. And the whole shidderee was all jumbled up inside me. And I couldn't make any headway on any of it.

I couldn't collect; I couldn't sell. I mean, sure, I collected and sold some but nothing like I should have. As for the other, well, the more I thought about that—and I couldn't stop thinking about it—the more mixed up I got.

You see? You've probably seen it. If there was ever a bastard that was going off half-cocked, I was it. I didn't know the layout of the house. I didn't know how long it would take Mona to get that dough out of the basement, or which room was her aunt's, or whether she'd let me into the place at night, or—or a goddamned thing. Worst of all, I hadn't laid the deal out for Mona. I hadn't rehearsed her in how she was supposed to act afterwards; what she was suppose to say and the story she was supposed to tell the cops and so on. I hadn't done it because I hadn't really planned on going through with the deal. I'd figured that Pete had skipped town, and I couldn't go through with it. So there it was. There I was. I hadn't asked Mona half the questions that I should have, and I'd told her practically nothing that she needed to know. And now it was too late. I didn't dare call her. There was no way I could see her. Maybe I could catch her outside the house if I hung around that neighborhood long enough. But that wouldn't look good: people might remember seeing me later. And anyway I didn't have the time.

Wait? Put it off a night or two until I got a chance to talk to her? I couldn't do that. There was that story I'd given Pete; and then the old woman might discover that the till had been tapped.

So there it was, like I say. I was fumbling before I even got started. I hadn't really made a move yet, and I'd already bollixed the frammis. Anyway, I hadn't done what I should have.

I got to thinking about that while I was whipping the dead-beats. Or trying to whip 'em, I should say. I thought, well, Dolly, you ain't changed a bit, have you? You haven't learned a goddamned thing, you stupid bastard. You couldn't learn a prayer at a revival meeting. You see something you want, and that's all you got eyes for. You ain't watching the road at all, and the first thing you know you're up to your tail in mud ...

Well, though, that wasn't so. It maybe looked that way, but it wasn't the way it really was. There's just some guys that get the breaks, and some that don't. And me, I guess you know the kind I am.

I got through the day somehow, and along toward quitting time my mind began to clear. I began to figure I hadn't done so badly after all. The money was there—wasn't it?—and I had Pete sold—didn't I?—and Mona would do what I told her to—wouldn't she? Everything important I'd taken care of fine; and all that was left was just a few little details. Of course, it would have been better if I could have explained things to Mona. But it didn't really matter. I'd done all right, and everything was going to be all right. It had to be, know what I mean? Take the most hard luck guy in the world, and he's bound to get a break once in a while.

I worked until after six, trying to make a showing. The other guys had already checked in and left when I went in; and Staples was back behind the cash wicket, fidgeting and waiting for me.

He looked through my sales contracts—the new ones and the ad-buys. He checked through my collection cards, and counted my cash.

"A little light, Frank," he purred, looking up at me at last. "Quite-some-much light. I trust you can bulk it out with a good story?"

"What the hell?" I said. "I've been off work for almost a week. It takes a few days to get back into the swing of things."

"No." He shook his head. "No, it doesn't, Frank. It takes exactly one day. Today. Do I make myself clear?"

"So all right," I said. "I'll do much better tomorrow."

"You will indeed. Much better. Otherwise, I am very much afraid that—"

I shrugged and told him to stop making a production out of it. If I didn't do okay tomorrow, he could beef then. So he let it go at that and we said goodnight, and I started for home.

I *would* do all right the next day. If I couldn't do it legit, I'd feed a little of that hundred grand into the accounts. Just a few bills, enough to make myself look good. I could afford it, with that much dough, and it would save me knocking myself out.

I got home. Pete was pretty uneasy from being cooped up all day; all set for another quiz program, it looked like. So I told him I had to take a bath and he was to fix the grub I'd brought home. And that got him off my neck for an hour.

We ate around seven-thirty. By eight, we were finished. I told him I had a little work on my accounts to do, and he was to wash the dishes. So that took care of him until eight-thirty.

He came out into the living room, then, and I folded up the collection cards I'd been playing with. I told him to get his hat and coat on, and he did—looking like he was about ready to pop. Then I gave him one of the two big drinks I had poured. And as soon as he got it down, I poured us another.

"Dillon, good friend. Dere is somet'ing—"

"Drink your drink," I said. "Hurry! We're running late."

"But—"

But he drank his drink, and I drank mine. I switched off the lights, took his elbow and started him toward the door in the darkness.

"It iss only a small t'ing, Dillon. Unimportant but it hass been running through my mind. Since last night, ven ve vere—"

"You hear me?" I said. "I said we were late. Now, come on."

He came along, but that question, whatever it was, was still bothering him. And all the way across town he was kind of mumbling and muttering to himself. I guess I told you that the house was out beyond the university, the only one in that block? Well, it was, anyway; sitting off by itself. But I still didn't take any chances. I speeded up a little at the end of the adjoining block, then cut my lights and motor and coasted the rest of the way.

I opened the door. I told Pete to stay in the car until I called him.

"Oh?" He turned and looked at me. "But I t'ought—"

"I know," I said, "but she might hear you come up on the porch. Figure that something screwy was going on, and it would blow the whole deal."

I left him sitting in the car, mumbling and muttering. I was about half way up the walk when I thought, what if someone should come by, a prowl car, and ask him what the hell he was doing. But ... well, I couldn't help it. It wasn't good, but it wasn't good to have him come up on the porch either like I'd told him to last night. That wasn't good and this wasn't—and maybe nothing could be that I would dream up. But goddammit, I just hadn't had much time to think, and I was a hard luck bastard to begin with, and ...

I knocked on the door, and, man, it just sounded like an echo from my heart. The old pump was beating that hard. After a long time—a dozen years, it seemed like—the old woman tipped the shade back and peered out at me.

There was only a dim light on in the hall where she was standing. But it was apparently enough for her to recognize me. She opened the door and unlatched the screen, and I went inside.

Her face fell a little when she saw I wasn't carrying anything. Then she jerked her head toward the door, and started grinning again. Rubbing her hands together.

"You bring my coat? You got it in your car, hah?"

I didn't say anything, do anything. I was like a mechanical man with the batteries run down. I wanted to boff hell out of the old bitch, and I just couldn't move.

"You bring it in, mister. That's why you came, ain't it? You bring in the coat, and then..." She winked and jerked her head toward the rear of the house. "She's already in bed, mister, and you just br—"

She just shouldn't have said that. Honest to God, I'd planned it and I'd already come three-fourths of the way. But if she hadn't've said that, I don't think I could have gone any further.

She brought it on herself when she said that. She asked for it.

And she got it.

I left-hooked her, I right-crossed her. I gave her just the two haymakers, left and right. Fast. Batting her one way, then the other. Batting her back before she could fall. And then I let her go down, back against the foot of the stairs; and her neck looked about four inches longer. And her head was swinging on it like a pumpkin on a vine.

Kill her? What the hell do you think it did?

Mona had been standing behind the living room drapes. Now, she came out, and she took just one look at the old woman and then she looked away again.

And she threw her arms around me, shivering.

I kissed her on top of the head, gave her a little squeeze. I pushed her out of the hall, into the living room.

"D-Dolly. What are we g-going to—"

"I'll tell you," I said. "I'll tell you exactly what to do. Now, which room is your aunt's?"

"A-at the head of the stairs. On the right. Oh, D-Dolly, I'm—"

"Save it," I said. "For God's sake save it! Where'll she have her key? Where's her key?"

"I d-don't—maybe in h-her—"

I ran out in the hall, and frisked the old woman. I found a key in her pocket and took it back into the living room.

"Is this it? Now, what about the gun? In her room? Goddammit, answer me!"

She nodded, stammered that the gun was in the old gal's room. She gulped and tried to smile, tried to get ahold of herself.

"I'm s-sorry, Dolly. I'll do whatever—"

"Swell," I said. "Sure, you will, and everything's going to be fine." I smiled back at her—did the best I could at smiling, anyway. "You go get the money, now—how long will it take you? Can you get it in five minutes?"

She said she could, she thought she could. She'd do it just as fast as she could. "But what are you—"

"Never mind, goddammit!" I said. "Just go get it, and leave the rest to me. Move, for God's sake!"

She moved. She turned and went off at a run.

I went back out into the hall, slung the old woman over my shoulder and carried her up the stairs.

I got to the top, and dropped her on the landing. I unlocked the door to her room, and went inside.

There was a chair, a bed, an old dropleaf writing desk. Nothing else. No books. *No pictures. And with an old house like this, an old woman like that, there should have been pictures* ...

I opened the dropleaf of the desk, scared sick that there wouldn't be any gun or that it wouldn't be loaded. And I thought, man, oh man, how stupid can you get? You could have checked on *that,* anyway. You've gone too far to back out, and if that gun isn't ... But it was there; a big old forty-five, of all things. Just about the last gun you'd expect an old woman to have. And it was loaded.

And there was some money, too; a little roll of bills in one of the desk drawers.

I took the money and shoved the gun into my belt. I jerked the drawers out and dropped them on the floor, and I knocked over the chair as I went back into the hall.

I walked down the stairs a few steps. I reached back up and got the old woman by an arm, and pulled her down head first.

I left her lying about half way down. I went on down the rest of the way, scattering the bills on the steps. I switched off the light, opened the door and called to Pete. Then, I went back up the stairs a little way and waited.

I was sweating like a chippie in church. It wouldn't work; it *couldn't* work. It was like some of those stupid jobs you read about in the newspapers. Guys tackling some big deal and doing everything bassackwards, tripping over their own feet in a hundred places until it's almost like a comedy. I'd read some of those stories, laughing out loud and shaking my head, thinking, what a jerk! The damned fool ought to have known, he ought to have seen: if he'd done any thinking at all, he'd—

The door opened. Closed. I heard him breathing heavily, nervously; and then his whisper in the darkness:

"Dillon? Vot—"

"Everything's swell." I spoke softly. "She's up in her room now writing the statement. I'm going up to check it over."

"Oh?" I could almost see the frown on his face. "Den vy am I—"

"I want you to look at it before we leave. It's okay. She won't know you're here until I get my hands on it."

"Vell," he said, hesitating, trying to unravel things. And then he gave it up and chuckled. I was his pal, I was the brain man. I was taking care of him, just like I'd been taking care of him. And he was a simple guy; and there was this other thing on his mind:

"... all day I haf been trying to remember, Dillon. Soch a crazy thing. How does it go, dot song ve vere singing: der vun about der bastard king of England?"

"*Song!*" I gasped. "*Song!*" Is that what—" I brought my voice down. "Turn on the light, Pete. I accidentally brushed the switch with my sleeve when—when—" *When what?* "You'll have to turn around. It's there on your right, back near the door."

I saw the black shadow that was his body revolve in the darkness. I heard his fingers tracing their way along the wallpaper. Then, the chuckle again, almost childish:

"... soch a foolish t'ing at a time like dis. No attention you should pay me. Later, perhaps, ven—"

"No," I said. "This is a good time. Here's the way it goes, Pete:

'*Cats on the rooftops, cats on the tiles,*

'Cats with their bottoms wreathed in smiles ...' "

The light went on. His back was to me like it had to be.

I got him six times through the head and neck. He pitched forward, and that was the end of him.

I made sure of it. I checked him before I left. His face was pretty much of a mess, but it looked like he'd died happy. It looked like he was grinning.

12

THROUGH THICK AND THIN: THE TRUE
STORY OF A MAN'S FIGHT AGAINST HIGH ODDS
AND LOW WOMEN ... by Knarf Nollid

I WAS BORN in New York City one score and ten
years ago, of poor but honest parents, and from my
earliest recollections I was out working and trying to
make something of myself and be somebody. But from
my earliest recollections someone was always trying
to give me a hard time. Like this time when I was
running errands for a delicatessen and, hell, I wouldn't
have stolen a damned dime from anyone: I was only
about eight years old and just wasn't smart enough.
So this old bag shortchanges me on an order, and the
delly owner says I took the dough myself. Well,
anyone could have seen she was a goddamned bag,
dirty dishes and clothes strung all over her apartment,
living like a hog. And later on she pulls the same stunt
on some other delivery boys around there, and everyone
gets wise to her and they know I didn't take the
money. Meanwhile, though, this delly owner has
canned me and told my old man I was a thief, and the
old man beats me black and blue.
   So a hell of a lot of good it does me.

That is one thing I can't figure out. Why your own parents will take some outsider's word for something before they will yours. But I realize that this incident is of no importance, so I will get on with my tale. I simply wished to demonstrate how right from the beginning people were giving me a bad time.

Well, it went on and on, and I will not trouble you with a full recital of it all. Because all the crap I caught, it's pretty hard to believe, and you'd probably think I was a damned liar.

So finally I'm in my second year of high school, and people have been giving me trouble all the way, trying to hold me back, and I'm pretty big not to be any further along. Anyway, there's this English teacher, and she's pretty young; not a hell of a lot older than I was, I guess. And she keeps giving me the eye and putting her hand on my shoulder when she shows me how to do something. And I figure, well, you know. So one day when she keeps me after class—it's the last class of the day and we're all alone—one day when she's leaning over me and kind of rubbing up against me, why I give her a feel. I thought she wanted it, you know, so I did it. But dear reader it was a trap.

Well, I suppose it was an invaluable lesson, and one that profited me greatly in the future. That little bitch taught me something I never forgot, *viz:* the prettier and the sweeter they act toward you, the less you can trust 'em. They're just leading you on, see, to get you in trouble. And maybe you don't see it right at the time, but, brother, you will.

But it was sure a lesson purchased at great cost. I get the chilly drizzles right now when I think about it.

She yells and slaps my face, and some of the men teachers come running in, and I try to explain how it was, what I thought, and that just makes it worse.

They call the principal, and they all start knocking me at once. It's their fault, see, that I'm not any further along. But they claim it's me. They give out with a lot of craperoo about how I won't study, I haven't really got my mind on school, and I'm uncooperative and antagonistic toward the other kids. And they make it sound like I'm public enemy number one or something; and it all started because this babe gave me a play, and I foolishly picked her up on it.

Well, to make a long story short, I got expelled and thus through no fault of my own, my formal education was terminated at a tender age. But to hell with 'em all, I say. People that act as dirty as that, they're not worth soiling my mind thinking about, and I don't.

You are aware by now that I am one hard working bastard with plenty of experience in many fields. But incredible as it seems, my earnest efforts and ability were never appreciated. The rookings I got right from the time I left home and took to the road are something to challenge the imagination. You'd have to see it to believe it, by God!

There was the manager of this circulation crew I first went out with. A crook from way back, and, man, what a crap artist. He gives me the old bull about traveling to California and back in new cars and making seventy-five bucks a week. And me, I'm just an innocent kid, unwise in the ways of the world, so I swallow it like candy. I sign on with the crew, there's about eight of us in this ten-year-old Dodge, and it seems like our first stop on our way to California is Newark, N.J. and—

You ever do the door-to-door in Newark? Well, don't do it. They get all the crews coming out of New York, see. These circulation outfits and so on, they shake the crews down in Jersey, and it's not really a fair test because the goddamned place is worked to death, but that's the way it is.

They shook out two of the guys in Newark, and another one before we're out of the state. Then, the rest of us go on westward, the crew manager and us four men. Well, I really knocked myself out. I made the doors and I made the sales. But it don't do me no good. It's like it's always been with me: working hard and being honest, and getting nothing for it. The crew manager, this bull artist, would do the call-backs on my orders, and on about two-thirds of 'em he'd give me a can't-confirm. He'd look me right in the eye and say the lady had changed her mind or her husband wouldn't let her go through with the buy. And then he'd write the orders up as his own and take the commission.

Well, we got into Illinois, and I'm practically dead of doughnut poisoning by that time. I've been working my can off, and all the time I have to eat in dumps, taking a lot of guff from the hired help just because I'm a kid and I can't tip or anything. So just about then I began to get wise. I made a few call-backs myself, and then I jumped this crap artist. I wasn't mean about it or anything. Just asked him how about shaking it out fair from now on. And that shows how little I knew of the ways of life. The son-of-a-bitch slugged me with a water pitcher, and then he kicked the hell out of me. And then he fired me off the crew. And I wanted to fight or argue about it or something, but somehow I just couldn't. Getting slugged and kicked when I'd been trying to be nice—well, I couldn't do anything for a while. Just hole up in my room and think.

Well, pretty soon I joined up with another crew, and inside of a month I was manager of it. Me, just a kid, managing a crew, so I guess you can see I had what it took. But there were a couple of these punks that were always kicking, hinting maybe that I was crapping them on the can't-confirms. So finally I got 'em alone in my room, and beat the sap out of them. And then I gave 'em the gate. But they still weren't satisfied. It wasn't enough that I had to go out and dig up a couple of more men. They wrote to the home office, and the next thing I know I'm yanked off the crew and I can't ever work for that company again.

It went on and on like that, every damn thing I tried. I work into a nice premium deal, and the superintendent robs me on territory. I buy gold, and the refinery gives me the cob; even the big buyers do it, by God. They try to kid me that my eighteen-karat is fourteen and that the fourteen is ten, and so on. And I'll bet I was skinned out of thousands of dollars before I saw I was struggling against hopeless odds, and moved into another racket.

It was that way with everything I did, the aluminum ware, the pots and pans, the premiums, the magazines: everything. One way or another, I'd get the blocks put to me; so I will mercifully spare you the sordid details. I often thought, I kept thinking, that if I had some little helpmeet to dwell with, the unequal struggle would not be so unequal. But I didn't have any more luck that way than I did in the others. Tramps, that's all I got. Three goddamned tramps in a row ... or maybe it was four or five, but it doesn't matter. It was like they were all the same person.

Finally, I was working in this small city in the middle-west. Outside collection-sales. It could have been pleasant and remunerative, but my boss was just about the most no-good son-of-a-bitch I ever worked for. Character named Staples. He just wasn't satisfied unless he was giving me a hard time, and when I go home at night, exhausted with the struggles ainst unequal odds, it's more of the same. Because the babe I'm married to then, she's out of this world, what I mean. The queen of the tramps, and a plenty tough bitch to boot.

To get ahead of myself a little, she starts giving me a hard time one night, talking dirty to me and using bad language. So like I always do, I try to be reasonable and show her the error of her ways. I say it is not the best time to talk when a man just comes home from work, and perhaps we will both be in a better mood after we have a bite to eat. I say, will she please fix us a bite, and I will cheerfully help her. Well, for answer she gives me some more of the dirty talk. And when I try to pet her and soothe her down, gently but firmly, she somehow slips and falls into the bathtub.

I helped her out and apologized, although I hadn't done a goddamned thing. "I'm very sorry, Joyce," I said. "Now, you just take it easy and I'll fix us a nice dinner ..." That's the way I talked to her, but you know how much good it does trying to be nice to a tramp. She almost caved my skull in with a scrubbing brush. Then, when I leave the house to calm myself, she ruins all my clothes and pulls out. I guess she saw that she couldn't get anything more out of me, and it was time to latch onto another sucker.

Meanwhile, to go back and take events in their proper order, I have met one of the sweetest, finest little girls in the world. Her name is Mona, and she lives with a mean old bitch of an aunt. The old woman's holding her prisoner, practically, working her tail off and making her do a lot of dirty things. She, this little girl, asks me to rescue her and let her be my helpmeet, and then we can live happily forever after. And touched by her plea, I agree to do so. I agree even before I know about all this dough the old woman had stashed away, which—when you come to think about it—is rightfully Mona's, because the old bitch has given her a hard time every day for years. And if a little girl ever had a hundred grand coming, she did.

Well, I go over to the house that night, and, hell, I wouldn't have laid a finger on that old woman. But she keeps egging me on, talking dirty and giving me a bad time. So there just wasn't any other way out.

Well, just about then, maybe a few minutes later, this fellow Pete Hendrickson came in. I think maybe he was a Nazi or maybe a Communist—one of 'em that slipped over here during the war. But, anyway, he was a no-good bastard; he admitted being a bum, himself. And he would have given me a hard time, too. So there was only one thing to do about him.

Well, I'd done it to him; and I was wearing gloves, but I wiped the gun off good and put it in the old woman's hand. And just as I'd finished, this Mona shows up with the money.

And she sees this Nazi or Communist or whatever he was, and she goes all to pieces. Acts like I was a criminal or something. Acted like I hadn't done it all for her.

Well, she pulled herself together when she saw how jarred I was, the notion I was getting. She said it was just a shock, seeing him there when she hadn't expected to, that she just didn't like to have it happen to anyone unless it was her aunt. And she was sorry and so on, and she'd do whatever I asked.

So I'm a pretty understanding guy, and I kind of liked her for feeling that way. *If* she did actually feel that way. So everything was jake between us again.

I told her what she was supposed to do, what to say to the cops. I told her it would be a leadpipe cinch, and in a couple of weeks we could get together. Then, I kissed her and left, taking the money with me.

It—the money, I mean—was in a black leather bag, something like a file-briefcase or a doctor's medicine kit. It was packed tight and it was heavy, about sixty or seventy pounds. And all the way home I was wondering where in the hell I could keep it. I was afraid to hide it in the house. That was a pretty bad neighborhood, and it would be just my luck to have some son-of-a-bitch break in and lift it. I finally decided to carry it with me, at least for a while. I could bury it down in the bottom of my sample case—throw out some of the samples if I had to—and keep it with me all day long.

I got home, and took it into the house. I set my sample case up on the coffee table, opened the lid and tried fitting the bag inside. I kind of fiddled around with it, trying it this way and that way. I was sort of delaying the pleasure, I guess, letting my anticipation build up. And I guess probably I was a little afraid. Because with a hard luck guy like me, damned near anything can happen. That little satchel might turn out to be filled with bricks or magazines. Or some kind of booby trap that would blow my head off when ...

I opened it. It bulged open the second I pressed the catch, and I made myself look inside. And I sort of moaned, nickered like a colt going for its mother.

It was there, all right. Packs and packs of paper-banded bills. Fives, tens, and twenties. I dipped my hands down into it, and brought them up again. And it was all money—no false packages, no junk: I didn't have to count it. Hell, I could almost count it in my head ... a hundred grand.

A hundred grand!

And Mona. I'd rescued her from her wicked aunt and meted out justice to this guy who had molested her, and I'd recovered this money which was rightfully hers. And soon we would shake the dust of this old land from our feet, depart this scene of my many tragic disappointments, and we would go to some sunny clime like Mexico. And, man, what a happy life we'd lead. Me and that sweet child, that honey babe, and a hundred thousand dollars.

Or practically a hundred thousand. I'd probably have to feed a few hundred into my accounts to keep Staples happy.

I dipped down into the money again, squeezing and rubbing it between my fingers, hating to let go of it. It was old, of course, but still clean and crisp. And, yeah, hell—you think I haven't been around?—it was the real thing. I make no pretense of being a great mental genius, but there is one thing I cannot be fooled on, dear reader. The green goods. I cannot be deceived about counterfeit. You get stuck a few times like I have, when you are an innocent, trusting kid, and have to make it up out of your own pocket. And you learn to spot the goddamned stuff a hundred yards away.

I took six bills, thirty dollars, from a packet of fives and stuffed them into my wallet. That would give me a good day at the store, and keep this unappreciative character, Staples, who was always giving me a hard time, from giving me a hard time.

I dropped the rest of the pack back into the satchel, and started to fasten the catch. And I was a happy man, dear reader. I had won out in the unequal struggle, with every son-of-a-bitch in the country, even my own father, giving me a bad time. I had forged onward and upward against unequal odds, my lips bloody but unbowed. And from now on it would be me and Mona and all this dough, living a dream life in some sunny clime—Mexico or Canada or somewhere— the rest of the goddamned world could go to hell.

But though I seldom complain, you have doubtless read between the lines and you know that I am one hard luck bastard. So, now, right as I stood on the doorstep of Dreams Come True, my whole world crumpled beneath me. I had all this dough and I had Mona—or I soon would have her—and then I looked up, and (TO BE CONTINUED).

... She was in her nightgown. She was all prettied up like I hadn't seen her since I don't know when; and she wasn't more than a dozen feet away. Standing in the entrance to the little hall that led back to the bedroom.

Smiling at me, but sort of watchful. Kind of smile-frowning.

Joyce.

My wife.

I DIDN'T THINK she'd seen the money. I wasn't sure, but the lid of the sample case was up, you know, and it wasn't likely that she would have.

I let it drop casually—the lid, I mean—and locked it. I said, "What the hell are you doing here?"

"I—" Her eyes flashed, but she held onto the smile—"I still had my key, Dolly."

"So you had a key," I said. "So suppose you had a nickel. You got to make a telephone call with it?"

"Please, Dolly. Don't make it any harder for me than it is."

"And you never made anything hard for me, did you?" I said. "You didn't do your goddamned best to wreck this house before you left. You didn't screw up every goddamned stitch of clothes I had. You didn't—"

"I know. I'm sorry, Dolly. But I've thought things over, and if you'll just listen to me—"

"Listen, hell," I said. "Listening to dames like you is what's put me where I am today." And then I shrugged and said, "All right, spill it. I'm listening."

I'd decided I'd better. Because maybe she *had* seen that dough, and anyway this was no time to get into a brawl. I had to live nice and quiet for the next few weeks. My nerves wouldn't take anything else, and anything else—anything that might draw attention to me—just wasn't safe.

She hesitated, looking at me, a little suspicious I guess of the sudden change. I said, "Well, come on. Give. Sit down and I'll get us a drink."

"I don't think I want a drink." She shook her head. "You've been drinking quite a bit, haven't you, Dolly? There's all kinds of bottles around and it looks like you slept in the bed with your shoes on. And—"

I was staring at her. Not saying anything, just staring. She cut off with the nagging fast, stretched her smile.

"Just listen to me, will you? I'm not back in the house an hour, and already I'm—you get us a drink, honey. Please."

I got a bottle out of the cupboard, and a couple of glasses. I came back into the living room; and she was sitting in the same chair Pete had sat in. And, well, it gave me an awfully funny feeling.

I poured the drinks and handed her one. My hands shook, and I patted the lounge at my side. "Why so unsociable? Why not sit over here?"

"We-el. You really want me to?"

"What the hell? Sure."

"Well—" She sat down on the lounge kind of crossways to me. "Well, here I am."

"Yeah," I said. "There you are, all right."

"I—I guess it would be too much to hope . . . I guess I shouldn't ask if you're glad to see me."

I let myself frown a little; thoughtful, you know. I took a sip of my drink, lighted a cigarette and passed her one.

"Well, it's kind of a funny deal," I said. "A guy's wife wrecks damned near everything he has, and then she takes off for a week—almost a week—and he thinks it's all over. He doesn't know where the hell she's been, what she's been doing with herself. She shows back up without any warning, and for all he knows—"

"I've been in Kansas City, Dolly. I'd started back to Houston; I was going to get my old job back—"

"Where'd you get the money?"

"From the owner of the club. I called him collect after I left here that night, and he wired me two hundred to get back on."

"Oh."

"No, Dolly. Please don't act like that, honey. You know I wouldn't—couldn't. You know there's never been anyone but you."

"I didn't say anything," I said. "So you stopped off in K.C., huh?"

"Yes, I had a four-hour layover there between trains, and then I was going on. But ..." She paused a moment, looking down into her glass. "I don't know quite how to put it, honey. Maybe it was getting off by myself for a while, being able to stand outside of things and look at them. I could see the whole picture that way, Dolly, the good and the bad, and it began to look a lot different to me. I began to wonder why things had turned out as they had. I wasn't sure that I should come back, but I felt that I should at least think about it. So ... so that's what I did. I took a room in Kansas City, and I really thought. For the first time in months, I suppose. It was quiet and peaceful, and there wasn't something to get me upset the minute I—"

"Like me, for example?"

"I've been more to blame than you, Dolly. Entirely to blame, I guess. I was responsible for the way I acted."

"Well," I said, "I'm not throwing anything up to you, understand, but as long as you mention the subject yourself I ... " I turned and looked at her, feeling the blood push up into my face. "What the hell you mean, *you* were responsible?"

"Please, honey. I'm here to help you. I love you and I'm your wife, and it's a wife's place to stick by her husband."

I poured myself another drink, the neck of the bottle rattling against the glass. I threw it down at a gulp, and it calmed me down a little bit, but only on the outside. It didn't change the way I felt.

"You think I'm crazy, is that it?" I said. "Well, it wouldn't be any goddamned wonder if I was. I've been knocking myself out for people almost from the time I began to walk, and all I got for it was a royal screwing. It's like it was a plot, almost. The whole goddamned world sitting up nights to figure out how to give me a hard time. Every bastard and son-of-a-bitch in the world working together to—to—"

I stopped. It was all true, by God, but somehow saying it out loud, saying it just then, it didn't sound so good.

"Well, anyway," I said. "You've got to admit I've had plenty of hard luck."

"Of course you have, dear. So have a lot of other people."

"A lot of other people, hell! You name me just one person that's got the rooking I've got. In his work and his home life and—"

I stopped myself again.

She slid over on the lounge, put one of her hands over mine. "You do see it, don't you, honey? And now that you understand and I understand, we can stop it before—We can do something about it."

I'd do something about it, all right. She may have thought she'd had a tough time before, but she hadn't seen anything yet. I'd have her run out of here inside of a week, long before Mona and I were due to get together.

"There's ... I don't want to upset you, honey, but there's something I want to ask."

"Yeah?" I said. "Well, go ahead."

"Maybe I'd better not. Not tonight. I'm sure you wouldn't—uh—"

"Come on. Spit it out."

"Well. About the money. I—*Dolly!*"

I let go of her wrist, grinned and gave it a little pat. It had been a dumb thing to do, to cut her off before she had a chance to say whatever she was going to. But I just hadn't been able to help myself.

"'Scuse, please," I said. "I guess seeing you in that nightgown I kind of lost my head. Now what about the money?"

"We-el ... nothing. Do you really like the gown, honey?"

"Love it. What about the money?"

She hesitated. Then, she smiled and shook her head. "Nothing, honey. No, really, it's nothing. I was just going to say that—uh—well, I had quite a bit of money left from cashing in my ticket and all. And—uh—of course, I'll have to pay it back, but we could use if for a while and ... "

She went on smiling at me, smiling into my eyes. And, of course, she was a goddamned liar like every other woman I'd ever known. But I couldn't be sure she was lying now.

"Well," I said, "I won't say I couldn't use a little extra money."

"I'll give it to you in the morning," she said. "Be

sure and remind me of it."

"Those deadbeats have really been giving me a time," I said. "The rotten bastards, you'd think they were trying to see how hard—Well, skip it. I must be beginning to sound like one long gripe."

"It's all right, darling. Don't ever be afraid to talk to me."

"Well, anyway," I said. "I caught up with a flock of 'em tonight. Pulled in a nice little wad of dough. Ought to make Staples act half way decent toward me for a change."

"Wonderful," she said. "I'm so glad for you, honey." And it seemed to me that her smile became a lot more real; the watchfulness went out of her.

She turned down another drink. I poured one for myself, and sat sipping it, thinking; and then I happened to look at her out of the corner of my eyes. And she was looking at me the same way, her head cocked to one side.

I laughed and she laughed. I set down my drink, and pulled her over on my lap.

I kissed her. Or, I guess you could say, she kissed me. She put her hands back of my head, and pulled my face down to hers. And I thought we weren't ever coming up for air, but you don't hear me kicking. She was a lot of woman, that Joyce. She had the face and she had the build. It wasn't hard to forget, for a little while, that she was just plain no-good and never would be.

She pulled away at last and lay back, smiling up at me, wiggling and breathing pretty hard as I made with the hands.

"Mmmm," she said, half closing her eyes. "Oh, Dolly, we are going to be happy, aren't we?"

"Hell," I said. "I'm happy right now."

"Do you really like my nightgown, honey? Tell me the truth, now."

"Huh-uh," I said. "I don't like it."

"Oh? Why, honey, I spent almost one whole afternoon picking it out, and I was just sure—"

"It covers you up," I said. "I don't like anything that covers you up."

She laughed and said, "Oh, you!" and gave me a little pinch. She pulled my head down again, and whispered in my ear. "I'll tell you something, honey. It's a new kind of gown. It ... comes off ... "

Well.

Well, afterwards—after she'd gone to sleep—I got up to get a drink of water. And on the way back to the bedroom, I locked the sample case and put the key in my pocket.

I got back into bed. I turned on my side, and closed my eyes. And it was as though a guard had been taken away from a gate, or a door suddenly thrown open, letting in a hundred images that I hadn't looked at until then—that I hadn't really looked at. Letting them all rush in at me at once. The old woman and Pete. The way she'd looked, the way he'd looked. Her head swinging like a pumpkin, her body sprawled on the stairs. His face—his face and neck, the way he'd chuckled when he asked me ...

I screamed. I flung myself up in bed, rocking and screaming. Because, Jesus, I hadn't wanted to do it, and I wouldn't ever have done it again. But now it was done, and there wasn't any way I could undo it. And, God, I'd be caught sure as hell. I'd just blundered my way through, and probably I'd done a hundred things that the cops could trace me on. Or if they weren't bright enough to catch up with me, Mona would probably do the job for them. She'd get scared and talk to save her own neck, and—

"Jesus!" I rocked back and forth, screaming and crying. "Oh, God Almighty. My God, God, God ... "

And then there was someone else saying, "My God. Oh, my God, darling ... " And Joyce was holding onto me, her body rocking with mine.

"I'm s-sorry," I said. "I—I—God, I'm sorry! I didn't mean it! I'm—"

"Lie down," she said. "Lie down, and mother will hold her boy. Mother's never going to go away and leave her boy again. She's going to stay right here and hold him close like this, and nothing can hurt him then; there's nothing to be afraid of. He's with mother, and he's safe, and mother will understand whatever ... w-whatever ... "

I got hold of myself, partly. I said, "I must have been having a nightmare. I—"

"There, there," she said. "It's all right. Everything's going to be all right, darling. He's going to lie down now, and ... there. There, there."

She pulled me back down. She moved her pillow up a little bit and moved mine down a little.

"There," she said. "No, baby; around this way. Tha-at's my boy! Now, down a little, just a little more ... and then closer, darling. Very close to mother ... "

And she drew me close.

And slid the gown down off her shoulders.

WELL, even a punching bag gets a rest once in a while. And now and then, usually right after I've been torn all to pieces, I get a little relief. Things will actually begin to look pretty good to me. I've been down as far as I can go, you see, so I start going back up again—kind of soaring. And man, when you catch me that way I'm a hard guy to stop.

...Joyce was up ahead of me the next morning. By the time I'd dressed she had breakfast waiting—and a good one, no kidding. And she didn't say a word about the night before. I'd been sort of worried about that; worried and kind of ashamed. But she didn't let out a peep about it, or let on like there'd been a thing out of the way. So that day was started off right, right from the beginning.

She kept a little of the money from her trip for groceries, and gave me the rest. She gave me a love pat now and then while she was waiting on me; and I got a big hug and a kiss when I was ready to leave.

"Notice anything?" she said, smiling up at me. "I've got a house dress on and my hair is combed and my face is made up, and ... Did you notice?"

I started to say, so what: you want me to shoot off some skyrockets? But it just wasn't that kind of morning, so I said, "You're darned right I noticed. You look swell, baby."

"You'll be right home tonight?"

"Well, sure," I said. "Why not? Why wouldn't I come right home?"

"I just wanted to know. So that I could have dinner ready."

"Something on your mind?" I said. "Anything bothering you?"

Her face fell a litle: at the tone of my voice, I figured. Then, she stood on tiptoe and kissed me again; and she said, laughing, "Yes. You. I've got you on my mind. Now, run along so I can get some work done."

I started for town. On the way in, I stopped and bought a newspaper. And I had a hard moment or two before I found the story, and made myself read it.

It was okay. It was swell. The case was so open-and-shut that it hadn't even made the front pages. It was back on page three, and there was only about half a column of it:

Mona had been in bed asleep, and had been awakened "by the sounds of struggle." At first "too terrified to investigate," she had finally forced herself to "when the sound of several shots was followed by a prolonged silence . . . Mrs. Farrell's niece identified Hendrickson as a one-time odd-jobs man in her aunt's employ. He had quit, swearing vengeance, she said, after a dispute over his wages. As police reconstructed the case, Hendrickson returned to the house last night—drinking and surly—and demanded payment of the disputed sum. Angered by the elderly woman's refusal, he gave her a near-fatal beating, robbed her and started to flee. Mrs. Farrell managed to follow him to the head of the stairs and shoot him. She then fell and broke her neck, although, it is believed, she would have died anyway as a result of the beating ...

"Police revealed that Hendrickson had a record of several arrests for drunkenness, disorderly conduct and battery. He recently completed a six months' jail sentence for assaulting an officer who was taking him into custody."

That was just about it, all that's important. Mona had recited her story just as I'd given it to her. And thank God, there weren't any pictures. If they'd gotten her picture and she hadn't kept her face covered—like she was crying, you know, like I'd told her to—I'd've had some questions to answer. Staples would have recognized her as the same girl who bailed me out of jail, and he'd've been mighty curious about it. He'd've wanted to know what I was to her and she to me, and just where was I last night at the time of the killings. And if I couldn't answer his questions—

But there weren't any pictures. The case was too open-and-shut. The people involved just weren't important enough.

I stopped at the store, and checked in and out. I went to work, trying to figure out some place where I might stash that dough. It was pretty awkward to lug around with me; heavy, and the samples didn't cover it too well. Lift up a few and there it was. Someone might accidentally spot it before I could stop 'em. Joyce might want some panties or stockings out of the case, and—well, any way you looked at it, it wasn't good to have it with me.

I thought about it all morning as I drove around. I fretted and fumed, trying to think of something, getting pretty sore at myself because I couldn't. But I couldn't, and that was that. I thought of a couple places, but they weren't any good. They were worse— or they seemed worse—than keeping the dough with me.

Check it at the railroad station? Well, you know how that is. Those guys are always banging stuff around, breaking stuff open accidentally-on-purpose. Or they give your baggage out to someone else. Or they get screwed up on the claim check, and you have to identify the contents ... You know. You read about it all the time.

A safety deposit box? Well, that would be just as bad, or more so. I'd have to give references to rent one—and maybe I could give Staples, huh? And, anyway, characters like me, we aren't supposed to have anything worth locking up.

I had to keep it with me. It was the only thing I knew to do. I'd just have to take the stuff out of the case that I was going to show people (and I wasn't going to show very damned much; I wasn't going to do very damned much work at all). As for Joyce, well, I could handle her. She was on her good behavior now, afraid of getting me sore, and I wouldn't need to give her any explanations or act apologetic. I'd just tell her to go down to the store if she wanted anything: I was tired of getting my samples screwed up. I'd keep the sample case locked, and tell her to keep the hell away from it. And if she didn't like it, she could lump it.

I framed the words in my mind, just how I'd tell her off if she started nosing around. And, then, I got to thinking about last night ... and I decided it wouldn't be necessary to talk to her that way. I'd say—well— I'd say, "Now, honey. I'm not even going to let your pretty fingers touch that junk. You just tell old Dolly what you want, and he'll bring you home something good."

It would be better to say something like that. It was just good sense, you know. Hell, you can still be polite to people even if you don't give a damn about 'em.

I knocked off work about one o'clock, and checked over my take. I had twenty-eight dollars—pretty good for a morning, but nothing at all for a day, of course. But with that other thirty, the six fives I'd taken from the hundred grand, it would make me a plenty good day.

I stopped in a bar. I ordered a pre-wrapped sandwich— those bastards could eat their own slop!—and a bottle of ale; and took it over to the booth. I ate and drank. I got another ale, and spread out my collection cards.

They were really honeys, these accounts we had. They made the first payment, and then you fought 'em for the rest. Catch those characters coming in or sending in the dough. You either fought 'em for it, or you didn't get it. And you didn't always get it then.

I picked out six past-dues, six accounts that owed us five bucks each. I marked them up on the cards, shifted the thirty from my wallet to the company cash bag, and, well, that was it.

It was about two o'clock by now. I moved on to another bar, buying a late paper on the way.

They'd cut the story down to about three paragraphs in this one. There was nothing new in it, or, rather nothing that mattered. The house and the furniture were just about the sum total of the old woman's estate. And it seemed like she was so far behind in her taxes that the property would just about cover 'em. She hadn't left any will. Mona was her only known survivor. And so on. Nothing that mattered. Everything was still okay.

I ordered my second double shot, and another ale for a chaser.

It was kind of funny about those taxes, the old woman not paying 'em. All that dough, and she'd let the taxes pile up until the county was on the point of taking over. But—well, maybe it wasn't so funny either. So strange, I mean. A lot of people don't pay taxes until the gun's right on them. And she'd been just as stingy and tight-fisted about everything else. Living on beans and junk. Making Mona lay for everyone that came along. She was just a miser, and there's no accounting for misers. The only money she'd spent that she could have got out of was that little bit of yard work she'd hired Pete to do. And—I guessed—she probably hadn't laid out much cash then. If any. Pete had taken it out in trade . . . got his pay from Mona.

Mona. She was a plenty sweet child, and I was in love with her. But I'd fallen in love before, thinking I was getting something special; and how had it turned out? How did I know it wouldn't turn out the same way with her?

I hadn't thought much about it until last night; hadn't had any real doubts about her. I'd been just a little bothered the way she'd cut loose with me. But except for last night I'd've been ready to skip it.

When you put the two together, the way she'd acted with me and the way she'd blown her top over Pete, and when you got to thinking about all those other guys . . .

Well, I wasn't putting up with any more tramps. I mean, I'd had enough goddamned tramps to last me a lifetime! I was sure that she wasn't one—pretty sure—but if I ever got the notion that she was, brother, look out!

What the hell could she do about it, anyway? What if I told her right now that she'd been on a buggy ride, and this was where she got off? Why she couldn't do anything, that's what. I could keep the money and tell her to go to hell—well, maybe I'd give her a few bills—and there wasn't a damned thing she could do about it.

And it wouldn't bother me that much.

If there's anything I can't stand, it's a goddamned tramp.

Joyce, now. Well, I've talked pretty rough about Joyce, and she *was* as lazy and sloppy and ornery as they come. But there was always one thing I was sure of—pretty sure—damned sure—regardless of what I said. She didn't play around. She never had, and she wouldn't know how to begin. It just wasn't in her, see?

If she'd been as square about other things as she'd been about that; if she kept up this act she'd been putting on since she'd been back ...

If it was an act. I figured it just about had to be, because a leopard don't change her spots. But it was a damned good one, as good as the real thing, so what the hell was the difference?

Joyce. Yeah, Joyce had her points all right. And now that I wouldn't have to knock myself out to make a living, now that I could feel like I amounted to something and we could have nice things, and—But that was the trouble. The money. How could I explain to her about the money? What kind of story could I hand her?

I guessed I couldn't explain; anyway, I couldn't think of a good story offhand. And there wasn't any hurry about it. I wasn't supposed to see Mona for a couple of weeks, and I could probably think of a lot of things between now and then.

Well ... I drank another round and left the place. I got some black coffee, and started driving again. Just around, just killing time. It was four o'clock. More than two hours before I could check in at the store, and get home to Joyce.

Joyce. Mona. Joyce? Mona?

What the hell? I thought, and I tried to push it out of my mind. Mona was a good kid. Anyone could see that she was; and she'd carried through on this deal like a little brick. Doing what she was told. Helping to murder her own aunt for her dough—

Well. Well, she was on the square, all right. She'd damned well better be. Because I *knew* Joyce was, and if I could just think up the right kind of story to account for that hundred grand ...

I drove around until after six, making myself look good. Then I checked in at the store, bustling in like I'd been on the run all day; and Staples' eyebrows went up a little when he saw what I had for him.

"Not bad, Frank," he said, counting the money. "Oh, not half bad. Perhaps by the end of the week you'll be doing a decent day's work again."

"Gee, thanks," I said. "You better watch that, Stape. You keep patting me on the back like that and you're liable to break your wrist."

He grinned down his nose. We said goodnight and I started to leave, and he called me back. "By the way, I see that a couple of your customers came to a violent end last night. One of your customers, I should say, and the relative of one."

"Yeah," I said, "I read about that. Too damned bad they don't all get bumped off."

"Oh, now, Frank. What would we do for customers?"

"I mean it," I said. "If every one of the rotten bastards dropped dead of the bleeding piles, it would tickle me pink."

"It really would, wouldn't it?" he nodded. "But this Farrell case. There's an angle of it which struck me as being rather curious."

"Yeah?" I said. "I mean, it did?"

"Mmm. Uh-hah. Mrs. Farrell was apparently a virtual pauper, yet her niece—her dependent—spends thirty-three dollars for a chest of silverware."

He stood looking at me, eyebrows cocked, waiting for me to say something.

I swallowed, and it sounded, by God, like Niagara Falls.

"Well?" I said. "What about it?"

"Frank! Honestly! And I've always looked upon you as my best man—in a hideous sort of way, of course . . . You actually don't see anything contradictory in the situation?"

"Well, I'll tell you," I said.

"Yes? Yes, Frank?"

"I'll tell you the way I feel, Stape. These bastards we got on our books, I don't try to figure them out. It's no use, know what I mean? You can't expect 'em to make any sense. If they weren't nutty as a pecan orchard they wouldn't be trading with us."

"We-el"—he hesitated—"yes. I can't say that I disagree with you. You'd attribute this, then, to merely another of the mental aberrations peculiar to our clientele? Spending their last dollar on—"

"Like I say," I said, "I don't think about 'em at all. Don't even try to figure them out. All I'm interested in is have they got the money, and can I get it away from 'em."

"Hear, hear!" He clapped his hands together. "Spoken like a true Pay-E-Zee man. Well, toodle-oo, dear boy, and pleasant dreams."

I started for the door again.

He called to me again.

"For God's sake!" I said, whirling around. "What the hell you want now, Stape? It ain't enough I knock myself out all day. I got to stand around here half the goddamned night talking to you."

"Why, Frank," he pouted. "I do believe you're annoyed with me! Is there something about this case that—uh—Did I say something that disturbed you?"

I told him sure he disturbed me. He bothered hell out of me. Hanging onto me this time of night when I wanted to get home and get my shoes off, and get some grub under my belt. "I've been working all day, know what I mean? I haven't been sitting around on my butt reading newspapers."

"I see," he nodded. "You feel a slight twinge of conscience. Mrs. Farrell tipped you off to Pete's whereabouts—didn't she?—and he no doubt guessed as much and—"

"So why should that bother me?" I said. "It all turned out all right. They both got killed."

He frowned, staring at me; turning a little pale. Then, he laughed, unwillingly, shaking his head.

"Oh, Frank," he said. "What will I ever do with you?"

"Keep me standing around here a while longer," I said, "and you won't have to do anything. I'll keel over from hunger."

"Unthinkable! ... 'Night, Frank."

"'Night, Stape," I said. And I headed for home.

He didn't know anything—didn't even guess anything. He was just staying in character, that was all, and I'd been stupid to get upset about it. Hell, hadn't he done the same thing a hundred times before? Picked at me; tried to rattle me! nosed around like a skunk in a garbage dump. Not because there was anything to act that way about, you understand. Just because he was the boss and you had to hold still for it, and being on the make himself he figured everyone else was.

Yeah, I should have counted on it tonight. He figured I'd had a hard day, and you could almost always count on it after a hard day.

So ...

So there wasn't anything to get up in the air about. Not a damned thing at all; and everything was jake. But still I was glad to get home. I was glad to have Joyce's arms around me, holding me tight; to hear her whisper that I was her boy—mother's boy—and she would never leave me again.

She held me, reaching up to stroke my head; and finally we sat down at the table side by side. It was all ready, the dinner I mean. She'd put it on the table when she heard my car. It was good and it was hot; and we sat next to each other, squeezing hands now and then. And I hadn't had much appetite before— hadn't thought I could eat a bite—but I really stowed it away.

She poured the coffee. I lighted two cigarettes, and gave her one.

"You asked me something last night," I said. "Now I'd like to tell you the answer."

"I'm glad, Dolly. I was hoping you would."

"You asked me if I was glad you'd come back. All I've got to say is you're damned right I am."

"Oh?" She hesitated. Then she leaned forward and kissed me. "I'm glad that you're glad, Dolly. It's wonderful to be back."

She cleared away the dishes, and I helped her. She didn't want me to, but I did, anyway. I wiped while she washed them; and then we moved into the living room. The light was turned down low. She curled up next to me on the lounge, her legs pulled up under her, her head resting against my shoulder.

It was pretty nice, mighty peaceful and pleasant. I felt like if it could just be this way forever, I wouldn't ask a damned thing more.

"Dolly," she said, and right at the same time I said, "Joyce." We spoke together, and then we laughed, and she said, "Go ahead, honey. What were you going to say?"

"Oh, nothing much," I said. "Probably nothing will come of it."

"Of what?"

"Well, it's a chance to make some real dough, a pile of it. Anyway, it looks like a good chance. One of the fellows down at the store, one of the collectors, well, his brother-in-law is manager of a big gambling house out in Las Vegas. And the owners of the place haven't been treating him right, see? He's made 'em rich, and now they're about to kick him out. So he wrote his brother-in-law, this collector down at the store, and told him that if he could get up some money, he—this manager—would place it with a shill, and let the shill win and—and—"

She hadn't said a word, hadn't changed her position. But all of a sudden the room seemed to have gotten cold, and her shoulder felt stiff against mine.

"Well," I said, "I guess maybe that isn't such a good idea. Might get in trouble on a deal like that. But there's another proposition I run across, and—"

"Dolly," she said. "I have to know. Where did you get that money?"

I LEANED forward and stamped out my cigarette in an ash tray. I stayed leaned forward while I lighted another one, and then I sat back again, and I yawned.

"Man, am I tired! You about ready to turn in, honey?"

"Dolly . . . "

"What?" I said. "Oh, the money! I thought I told you about that. I caught a few old accounts at home last night, people that really owed us a wad, and—"

"I saw it, Dolly. I don't know how much there was, but I know there was a lot. A whole bag full."

I turned around and stared at her. I gave her the hard eye, trying to stare her down, and she didn't flinch. There was a little frown on her forehead, but it wasn't unfriendly. She didn't look tough or like she might get tough. If she'd been that way, I'd've known what to do. But the way it was, I didn't. I couldn't've slugged her if I'd been paid to.

I couldn't do anything.

The silence must have gone on for five minutes. Finally, she reached out and took one of my hands in hers. And spoke.

"I came back to you, Dolly. It wasn't easy after everything that had happened between us, but I felt that I had to. I loved you and I wanted to help you."

"Well," I said, "you don't hear me kicking, do you?"

"Do you remember last night, honey? Don't you think that after that—d-don't you know that I love you and you can trust me, and that all I want is to help you?"

"I tell you," I said. "I'll bet we get waked up pretty early in the morning. I notice they've got a couple of cars of gravel switched onto the siding out here, and they'll probably be hooking onto 'em—"

She stood up, smoothed down her house dress. She looked down at me, frowning slightly; gave me a little nod like a teacher dismissing a kid.

"All right, Dolly. I guess there's nothing more I can say. Perhaps it's my fault for leaving you, going off in a tantrum when I should have known that you were— that a man who acted as you did was—wasn't himself and might ... Oh, Dolly! *Dolly!* What have you d-done ...?"

She threw her hands over her face and sat down on the lounge again, crying. Sobbing helplessly. And she seemed so alone, as lost and scared as I'd been last night.

"Joyce," I said. "Please, baby. What the hell? What are you acting that way for?"

"Y-you ... you know why. A-all that money—I hoped you'd tell me, that there'd be some innocent explanation. I d-didn't know what it c-could be, but I hoped. And now I know that you can't explain. Y-you're afraid, and—"

"Aw, now, wait a minute," I said. "Wait just a minute, baby."

I tried to pull her onto my lap. She moved her shoulders, shaking off my hands.

I waited a minute, looking at her, listening to her.

Feeling myself come apart inside. Then, I tried again, and that time I made it.

"I wanted to tell you about it," I said. "But I wasn't sure I was going to get to keep it, see, so I thought I'd better hold off a few days. Otherwise you'd be counting on it, and then you'd be disappointed."

"I d-don't ... " She pulled her head away from my chest and looked at me. "What—how do you mean—?"

"I found that money."

"Oh, Dolly!" She started to cry again. "Please. Not any more, I j-just can't stand it if you lie to me any—"

"I'm not lying. I know it sounds crazy as hell; I could hardly believe it myself. But it's true."

"B-but it—"

"I'm telling you. I'll tell you if you give me a chance. You want me to tell you or not?"

She sniffled, and looked at me again. I thought she was never going to stop looking, but finally she nodded.

"A-all right, Dolly. But p-please don't—if it isn't true, d-don't—"

"Well," I said. "I can't guarantee that you'll believe me. I've been afraid that no one would believe me, and that's what makes it so hard to know what to do."

"I w-want to believe you, honey. There's nothing I want more."

"Well, it happened last night. One of my accounts— a skip named Estill—I got a tip that he was living out on West Agnew Street. So I beat it out there, and the house was empty. If he'd ever lived in the place, he wasn't any more. Well, I got my flash out of the car and went inside, and—"

"Went inside?" She frowned. "Why?"

"Why?" I said. "Well, you'd know if you'd ever done any collecting, honey; if you'd ever worked for an outfit like Pay-E-Zee. We always go in if we can get in. You might pick up a telephone number off the wall, you know, or maybe there's been an old letter left behind. Something that will give you a lead on the skip."

"Oh," she said; and her frown faded and some of the doubt went out of her eyes. "Go on, honey."

"So I went in, and I looked around from room to room and I couldn't find a thing. Not a scrap of paper, or an address or nothing. It looked like—well, it almost looked like someone had gone to a lot of trouble to see that nothing was left behind. Like everything had been washed and scrubbed before they left. It was very screwy, know what I mean? It got me curious. So I kept on looking, and finally I found this—this little satchel, pushed way back on the shelf on one of the bedroom closets. I opened it up and looked inside, and I'm telling you, honey, it really threw me for a loop..."

I paused to light a cigarette. I offered her one—giving her a quick size-up—and I took a long deep breath. She'd swallowed it all, so far. It was a pretty good yarn, and she was anxious to swallow it.

"What did you say this man's name was, honey? This man you were tracing when—"

"Estill, Robert Estill. I've got his card right here in my pocket if you want to look at it."

She said, oh, no; but she hesitated a second first. So I took the card out and showed it to her. It was on the level—actually his card—which was a hell of a lot more than I could say for him. We'd got two payments out of him, and then he'd done the disappearing act.

"I can show you the empty house, too," I said—and I could have shown one to her. "It's at 1825 West Agnew, and I can drive you out there right now."

"N-no, that's not necessary. I—How much money is

there, Dolly?"

I started to lie, to tell her there was five or ten grand or some such figure. Because she might ride along with that where she might not with more. And once she'd started riding, the rest would be fairly simple. I could say—well, I could pretend like I'd invested part of the dough. Or gambled with it. Or—or done something to make myself a pile.

But she wasn't completely sold, yet. Not so sold, anyway, that it wouldn't be awfully easy to unsell her. If she asked to look at the money, to count it—

I told her the truth.

She jumped and almost fell off my lap.

"Dolly! Oh, my goodness, honey! A h-hundred thous—It must have been stolen! Or it could be kidnap money, or—"

"It's not marked," I said. "I know that. I checked it over, but good!"

"It's bound to be something like that! It just has to be. You've got to take it to the police, Dolly!"

"And suppose there is something shady about it— like there probably is? Where does that leave me, a guy like me—a floater with no friends or background? I'll tell you what would happen. If they couldn't beat me into signing some kind of confession, they'd just lock me up and keep me until they could dig up the right answers."

"But if you took the money in, that should prove that—"

"I tell you, they'd never believe me! They'd think I just got scared and was trying to do a cover-up. That's what makes it so hard, why I've been so worried. I won't say that I don't want to keep it, but what difference would it make if I didn't? The story sounds screwy. I can hardly believe it myself, and I don't reckon you believe it and—"

I shoved her off my lap suddenly. I went into the kitchen and reached a pint out of the cupboard, and I took a long stiff slug from the bottle.

I'd thought of something right while I was talking to her, something about the money. And it had rattled me like lightning on a tin roof. The dough wasn't marked, I knew that. But suppose there was something actually shady about it, that it actually hadn't belonged to the old woman? Suppose the cops or the FBI were on the lookout for certain serial numbers ...

I shivered. Then I remembered ... and I sighed with relief. Mona had bailed me out of jail with part of the money four days ago. If the stuff was hot, I'd have known about it by now.

I put the bottle back in the cupboard. I turned back around, and Joyce was there and she threw her arms around me.

"I believe you, Dolly," she said, her voice sort of desperate. "I believe every word of it."

"Well, gosh," I said, "I'll be frank with you, honey. I wouldn't blame you much if you didn't."

"W-what are you going to do, Dolly? We can't keep it."

"Well I don't know," I said. "I mean, what else can we do? I won't say that I don't want to keep it, but even if—"

"No! Oh, no, honey. There must be some way to—to—"

"How? You name some way where I won't have to go to jail, and probably get loused up for the rest of my life."

"We-el. Well, couldn't you go out to that neighborhood and make some inquiries? Find out—"

"Huh-uh! Attract a lot of attention to myself, and

maybe have someone call the cops? Not me. I was out there after dark and no one saw me. I'm in the clear so far and that's where I'm staying."

"But we just c-can't—"

"So tell me what we can do," I said. "Just tell me and I'll do it. You don't want me to go to jail, do you?"

"N-no. Oh, no, dear."

"If I thought it would do any good," I said, "I would. But all I can see is getting fouled up. It wouldn't help anyone. That much money, if it was stolen it must have been insured and the insurance money's already been paid over. No one's out anything but the insurance companies, and you know those birds. They already got half the money in the world. Got it from gypping people—foreclosing on farms and giving everybody a hard time. I see no reason why I should stick my neck out for some thieving insurance company."

She was silent. Thinking.

I stooped down and kissed her on top of the head.

"You and me, Joyce," I said. "We never really had a chance, honey. It was always one goddamned dump after another, never having a nickel to spare . . . Hell, I tell you. You may try hard—you may patch things up temporarily—but you go on living like that, and sooner or later . . . "

Her arms tightened. She whispered, "Oh, Dolly. Oh, I love you so much, honey."

"A hundred thousand," I said softly, "and it belongs to us just as much as it belongs to anyone. A hundred thousand . . . A decent house. A place with lots of windows so that the sunlight could stream in, and . . . and decent furniture instead of junk. And a good car for a change. And no worries. Not being half out of your mind all the time, wondering how the hell to make both ends meet. And—"

"And—?" she whispered.

"Well, sure," I said. "Why not? I'm all in favor of kids, if people can take care of 'em."

She sighed and hugged me closer.

"I knew you'd feel that way, honey. You were always so good about so many things, I don't know why I ever thought that—that—"

Her voice trailed off.

I waited, stroking her hair.

"I don't know, Dolly. I want to—I want to so much—"

"Why don't you look at it," I said. "Feel it. Count it. Let's count it together, honey, figure out how we can spend it. Like to do that, huh?"

"Well—" She hesitated. "No! No, I'd better not. It's hard enough to think straight as it is. Let's—let's just not talk about it any more. Let's ... let's ... "

So we didn't talk about it any more.

I picked her up in my arms, and carried her into the bedroom.

16

I HAD a good night.

I got off to a good start the next morning. Joyce was pretty thoughtful and a shade pale around the gills, as the saying is, but that was the way it should be. She was a swell kid—always been on the level and all—and naturally something that wasn't strictly kosher would give her a jolt.

I bought a paper on the way into town. I had to turn through it twice before I found the story about—well, you know—and it wasn't really about that, then. It was just mentioned in passing in connection with a little squib about the old woman's estate.

The county was filing a suit for the back taxes. Mona had been served with a thirty-day eviction notice.

I threw the paper away. I drove on to the store, thinking that the poor kid really wasn't getting any breaks. If the property had been clear, she might have got a nice piece of change for it. Enough to live on a couple years and make a new start somewhere. But it just wasn't in the cards; she was just the original hard luck kid. Of course, I'd give her a few bills—I wouldn't let her be put out on the street with no clothes and not a dime to her name. But it would have been a lot better if she'd had some real dough.

I wondered if she had any money to eat on, and I thought for a minute of slipping a few bills in an envelope and sending it to her. I felt sorry for the kid and I really wanted to help her, you know. But I finally decided against it. The police might be keeping an eye on the place. With all I had to lose, I wasn't taking any chances.

She'd get by all right. The way she was used to living, she probably wouldn't feel right if she had enough to eat.

Staples usually opened the store at eight-thirty, a half hour before I and the other outside men went to work. But he hadn't done it that morning. It was a few minutes before nine when I got there, and the place was still closed up tight. And the other guys were waiting out front for him to show.

I got out of my car and joined them. We waited around, smoking and talking, wondering if the son-of-a-bitch had got run over by a truck and hoping to hell that he had. But there was no such luck, of course. At nine-thirty, he showed up.

He unlocked, and we followed him inside. It didn't seem to be done deliberately, but somehow the other guys were all checked out ahead of me, and I was left alone with him. He began checking me out, kidding and laughing. I felt myself getting uneasy.

He just wasn't himself, know what I mean? He was in too damned good a humor. Well, sure, he was always ribbing and making with the fast talk, but it wasn't because he was Mr. Gayheart, scattering pearls of joy and so on. It was about as genuine as a dime-store diamond. He couldn't work you over with a ballbat, like he wanted to, so he swung the old needle. Making like it was a joke in case you got sore.

This morning, though, it was different. The son-of-a-bitch was really tickled pink about something.

I picked up my cards, and asked him what the big joke was.

"I'll bet I know," I said. "You tripped a blind man on your way to work."

"Ah, Frank," he giggled, giving me a pussy-cat tap on the wrist. "Always putting others in your place. As a matter of fact, I paid a call on an old friend. Someone I hadn't seen in almost twenty years."

"No kidding," I said. "You mean you go out to this nut house—they got you inside—and then they let you go?"

He giggled again, made another pass at my wrist. "You're getting warm, dear boy. Strange how our minds seem to run in the same sewer. The friend I visited, the acquaintance I should say, *was* in a public institution."

"Jail, huh? I knew it," I said. "Well, it's a good thing you've got a stand-in with the local cops."

"A stand-in I've gone to some pains to develop, Frank. It proves very useful in a position such as mine. But, no—you're still a little wide of the mark. It wasn't actually jail. More of a corollary establishment, I should say."

"Yeah?"

"Mmmm. An adjunct to the jail . . . But I see that I'm boring you, and I've already delayed you unpardonably. Away with you, good friend! On to the assault on the heels, and may their Achilles heel be bared to you."

"I don't dig this," I said. "This party you visited— he was in some kind of trouble?"

"No—ha, ha—I wouldn't say that, Frank. At least, the party made no complaint to me."

"Well, hell, then. What—"

"No—" He held up a hand. "No, I won't let you, Frank. You're just being polite, pretending an interest in my poor conversation, and I can't allow it. Do run along, now, I insist on it. And—oh, yes ... "

"I know," I said. "I know. You want me to knock 'em dead again."

"Knock them—? Oh, well put! Oh very well put," and he grinned.

I turned my back on him and walked out.

My stomach was all tight and funny feeling. It seemed to be narrowed, drawn down at the bottom, like I'd swallowed something heavy. And there was a sickish feeling in my throat, and hot-icy needles were jabbing through my head.

I got in my car, so shaky that I could hardly turn the switch key. I backed away from the curb and started driving, aimlessly, sort of blind. Finally, I pulled up at a bar, and parked myself in a rear booth.

The drink helped. The drinks helped. I began to calm down.

He couldn't know anything. The cops didn't, so how could he; and what the hell? Somehow he'd spotted that I was a little uneasy. He'd seen it and started working on it, trying to needle out the answer. He was swinging every which way, throwing out the scatter shots in the hope that one of them would hit something.

This frammis this morning, now; it just about had to be a dammed lie, when you started studying it. An ordinary guy would have come right out and admitted that he overslept or got stuck in an elevator, or something of the kind. But Staples wasn't an ordinary guy—a decent one, I mean. He'd lie just for the hell of it. Climb a tree to lie when he could stand on the ground and tell the truth. So, since he wanted to needle me anyway, he'd come up with this story about visiting an old friend.

A friend that wasn't anywhere, know what I mean? No place I could pin down. No place that I could check on if I took a notion. The party was in jail, but he wasn't—and so on. A big mystery. A lot of double talk.

If he just hadn't been so damned tickled, so pleased with himself ... but that would be part of the act, another scatter shot. Or maybe he had actually screwed someone, and it had put him in a good humor. He'd been boasting around about how he was going to make one of the maids at his hotel. He'd been working on it for weeks, hinting that he was going to get her fired, then turning the other way, sweetening her up with little presents from the store. So maybe he'd finally connected.

Anyway ...

Anyway, he didn't know anything.

DAMMIT, HE DIDN'T KNOW ANYTHING!

But I sure didn't feel like working. I couldn't whip the deadbeats today. If I tackled 'em the way I felt, they'd probably wind up collecting from me.

What I wanted to do was go home. Not do anything, you know, but just be there; stay there all day close to Joyce. But, hell, it was out of the question. She was already plenty bothered about the money, so upset that she hadn't even wanted me to leave it there in the house with her. She was about ready to go along with keeping it, instead of going to the police, but she still didn't like it. And if I laid off today she'd realize that there was a lot more not to like than she knew about.

I had four or five drinks in that bar, stretching them out until around noon. Then, I went back to my car and started driving again.

I drove to the outskirts of town, and turned off on a dirt road. I parked. I leaned over the seat, and opened my sample case.

I took twelve of the five-dollar bills this time. Enough to add up to a full day's work. I fingered them hesitating, thinking, and then I put six of them back and took three tens instead.

That was more like it. Twelve fives and nothing else might look a little funny.

I put the bills in my cash bag.

I spread the collection cards out on my clip-board, and doctored them.

Then ... well, that was all. There was nothing left to do, and I had almost five hours to do it in.

A picture show? Hell, who wanted to go to a picture show ... sit there in the dark ... alone. I could have enjoyed reading, because I'm quite a reader, see. But I couldn't sit out on the street and do it, and there's never a damned thing worth reading in these libraries. No good confession stories or movie magazines, or anything interesting.

I started driving again.

I guess there's nothing that'll get you down so fast as driving when you've got no place to go.

I kept thinking how nice it would be to go home—knowing it was out of the question—and I began to get pretty sore. What the hell, anyway? A guy's sick and worried and he can't even go to his own home, talk to his own wife. It was a pretty damned sorry state of affairs, if you asked me. A man knocks himself out—puts himself on the spot on account of her—and she keeps right on giving him a hard time. Banging his ears and worrying him, as if he didn't have enough to worry about already.

Mona wouldn't act like that. That little Mona, now, there was a real sweet kid, a real honey. She'd had to do a few things that she shouldn't have done, so maybe she wasn't high-class like Joyce . . . like Joyce pretended to be. But—

Huh-uh: about Joyce. Joyce wasn't much good at pretending; she'd told me off plenty of times in the past. The way she acted was the way she felt, and no put-on about it. But—Mona was okay, too, and I needed to see her, I needed to be with someone, talk to someone.

Someone—almost anyone—that was on my side.

I drove across town to that center where she sometimes shopped. I went into the little bar there, next to the drugstore, and sat down near the door.

It was one of those places: the kind that makes you wonder how the hell they stay in business. Because this joint, it sure didn't have any. An old codger nursing a dime beer. Some painted-up dame getting high on sherry, and counting her change every two minutes . . . That's all there was.

I had a couple of double Scotches. I told the bartender to pick himself up a buck tip, and I thought he was going to drop dead.

He set a bowl of peanuts in front of me. He dropped a handful of slugs into the jukebox. I told him the light up front was pretty bright and would he mind turning it off. Or, rather, I started to tell him. He had it turned off before I could finish the sentence.

"Okay? Anything else, sir?"

"I'll let you know," I said. And he took the hint and left me alone.

I turned a little sidewise on my stool. I sat looking up front, one elbow on the bar, drinking and thinking. And the time loafed by.

I bought another drink, and the bartender bought me one. I took a swallow or two from it, glanced at my watch. It was a few minutes after three. Probably she wouldn't be by. You never can see people when you really want to, so probably I wouldn't get to see her.

I got up and went back to the john. I came out . . . and there she was, just going by. I just got a glimpse of her. I sauntered up to the door, like I wanted to get a breath of air.

She went into the super market. I waited a couple of minutes, and then I went back to my stool. I stood by it, sipping my drink and watching the door out of the corner of my eye.

The jukebox had run out of slugs. The dame and the old codger had left. It was quiet in there and kind of echo-y, and I heard her—heard those fast footsteps of hers—before I saw her. I got to the door, just as she was passing. And, yeah, I let her pass.

I wanted to talk to her, but there was something I wanted worse. Something I wanted to know. So I let her go right on by, and stood in the door watching.

I watched her until she rounded the corner, two blocks away. I watched her and the cars on the street, the people, and then she was out of sight; and I felt a hell of a lot better. She wasn't being tailed. The police weren't keeping an eye on her. She was in the clear, which meant I was. So that jerk, Staples, could take his goddamned needle and . . .

I went back to my stool, kind of sorry that I hadn't got to talk to her—because she was a swell kid, you know—but glad that I'd handled it this way. Now, I was *sure,* and now I didn't need to talk to her. I was feeling okay, and I had the biggest part of the day licked.

I motioned to the bartender. He made with the whiz and the soda. I took out a cigarette, and he lit it for me, smirking and giving me the wink.

"Quite a dish, huh, sir? A really well-stacked babe."

"What?" I said. "What babe?"

"You didn't notice her, the one that just went by? Pretty little girl with so much above the belt she can hardly see over it?"

"Oh, her," I said. "Yeah, I believe I did notice her. Went by when I was getting some air, didn't she?"

"That's the one. Lives around here someplace, I guess. A real hot customer from all I hear."

"No kidding?" I said. "I thought she looked like a pretty nice girl."

"Well, you know the saying, mister. The nicer they look, the lower down they are. I—"

He caught my eye, and broke off. He began scrubbing the counter with the bar-towel, his smirk drawing in around the edges.

"Of course, I don't really know anything," he said. "All I've got to go on is what some of the fellows around here have said. Could be a lot of lies, and probably is."

I took another swallow of my drink. I said, well, I didn't know about that. "The way I figure, where there's so much smoke there's got to be fire."

"Well ... " His smirk started to spread again.

"She didn't get them breastworks from chinning herself. I wonder how a guy would go about getting some?"

"Well, they tell me it's pretty simple. From what I hear—and I got no reason to doubt it—all you got to do is give her the old proposition."

"Yeah? Just like that, huh?"

"So they tell me. They tell me it's just a matter of howsabout it, toots, and you can get out the coal shovel."

He nodded, giving me another wink.

I picked up my change—every damned penny of

it—and left.

I drove around a while, got myself some coffee and ate a handful of mints. It was that time, by then, so I went to the store and checked in. There was no hurrahing or needling from Staples. He had a dinner date, I guess, or maybe he'd decided that there wasn't anything he could nose out. Anyway, he checked me out fast, and I went home.

Everything was about like it had been the night before. A good dinner; Joyce being sweet and nice despite the way she was worried about the money. I couldn't think of much to say to her talk, so I just let her ramble on. At one time I got to frowning, unconsciously, staring around the living room and frowning. I wasn't really thinking about it at all, you know, but she thought I was.

"I'm sorry, darling," she apologized. "I've been meaning to clean house from top to bottom, but I've been so—well, never mind. I'll get busy on it the first thing in the morning. You won't know the place when you get home."

"Oh, hell," I said. "Let it go. It looks okay to me."

"No," she said, "I'm going to do it. It'll help to take my mind off of ... of ... " She didn't finish.

The next day was Thursday. Like the other days since Joyce had come back, it started off good. Breakfast was ready and waiting for me. Joyce was swell. There was no mention of the mur—of the case—in the morning papers.

I thought, well, everything else is so good, that goddamned Staples will probably give me a hard time. But I was dead wrong about it. I was the first guy he checked out, and he didn't waste any time about it.

I went back around the corner, and climbed into my car. I backed away from the curb, and—

I don't know where she'd been hiding, waiting. Back in some doorway, I guess. But suddenly there she was—Mona was—piling into the car with me. Stammering scared. So scared that I could hardly understand her.

"S-something's w-wrong, D-Dolly! T-t-the p-police are f-f-following me ... "

17

THE POLICE! Great God, the police were after her and she'd led them right to me!

My foot slipped off the clutch, and the car leaped forward. I jammed my foot down on the gas. Inside of two blocks I was doing seventy, right through the early morning traffic, and God, I don't know how I kept from being pinched or from smashing into someone. Then, I began to think again, and I slapped on the brakes. But I didn't stop.

The hell the police were following her! I knew damned well they weren't. But I wanted to get her away from the store neighborhood. If Staples saw us together, it would be just as bad as if the police were on our tail.

"Now, what's this all about?" I said, finally, heading the car toward the country. "I know the police aren't watching you. I *know,* see."

I told her about the afternoon before, how I'd wanted to see her but I wasn't the kind of guy to give way to my emotions. The important thing was to take care of her, make sure that everything was okay. So I'd taken time off from my job, gone to all kinds of trouble, and done it.

"B-but they don't do it in the daytime, Dolly. J-just

at n-night. Tuesday night and last night. I was afraid to call you or g-go to your house, and I knew you wouldn't be there during the day, s-so ... "

Well, that was a break. It would have been a hell of a note if she'd come busting in on me and Joyce.

"Never mind," I said, pretty damned disgusted with her. "Never mind the trimmings. You say the police have been watching you. How do you know they were police?"

"W-well, I—" She hesitated. "I d-don't know, but I supposed—"

"Tell me what happened. Start with Tuesday night."

"Well, I—I was just going out for a walk, Dolly. That house ... I get so scared in it now. I've hardly been able to sleep s-since—"

"Never mind, dammit. Just tell me what happened."

"This car. It was p-parked up at the next corner. Right where they—whoever was in it—could watch the house. And just before I got to it they turned the lights on me. I went on by and they started up—I m-mean, the car started up. It turned around in the street and began to follow me. I walked five or six blocks and it followed me until I turned the corner to go home."

"Well?" I said.

"Well—" She looked at me, looking like I was supposed to turn flipflops or something. "Well, I went for a walk again last night, and the same car was there. It was over on the other side of the street and they didn't turn the lights on, a-and—and I started walking pretty fast, so I didn't hear it when it started up. But I'd only gone a block when—"

"Yeah, sure," I said. "Oh, sure. And it followed you back to the corner again?"

"Yes. Well, no, not quite. You see, there were quite a few cars passing and—"

"I see," I said. And, boy, did I want to paste her. Scaring hell out of me; coming down around the store where Staples might have seen her. "Are you even sure that it was the same car? What kind of car was it, anyway?"

"I—I d-don't know. I don't know much about cars. I t-think it was the same as this one."

"You do, huh?" I said. "And do you know how many cars there are like this one on the road? Well, I'll tell you. Just about eight million!"

"Then you don't t-think—?"

I shook my head. I couldn't trust myself to speak. She saw how I felt, apparently, and she shut up, too.

Stupid. How stupid could you get, anyway? It wasn't enough that she was a tramp, she had to be stupid on top of it.

There were a lot of college guys out in that section of town. One of 'em—or some guy—had tried to pick her up. He sees a swell-looking kid out by herself at night, so he follows her, thinking she'll give him a tumble. And all he'd have to do was say how about it, toots, and she'd probably have jumped into his car. But he didn't know that, so . . .

Well, anyway, that's what had happened. Something of the kind. It had given her a hell of a jolt, naturally, being scared and having a guilty conscience and having to stay in that house where everything had happened. But still she shouldn't have acted like this. This was a hell of a stupid way to act.

I drove along toward the country, calming down. I began to feel sorry for her, to think that I couldn't really blame her for losing her head. It might have jarred anyone that was in the spot she was in. Even me, I might have been jarred myself. And I'm a guy that's used to taking it.

I started talking again, dropping in a sweet word now and then. I explained to her what had happened—that there wasn't a thing in the world to be scared about. She couldn't believe it at first. She'd been knocked for such a loop that she couldn't see the truth when it was pointed out to her. And proved to her. But I went on talking, and finally she did.

We were in the country by then. I turned off the highway, and parked. She leaned toward me a little, smiling kind of timidly. I put my arms around her. The coat she had on was worn thin, and all she had on underneath was one of those wraparounds. I could feel her, the warmth and the softness.

"Well?" I put my mouth to her ear and whispered. "Howzabout it, toots?"

"W-what? Oh," she said, and she blushed. "You mean here—in the d-daytime."

"What the hell?" I said. "You know the score. You ought to know it, anyway."

She didn't say anything, but something happened to her eyes. They went sick, so sick, as sick as a sick dog's. And I moved my hands away from where they had been, and just hugged her tight around the shoulders.

"I'm sorry," I said. "I talk pretty rough, you know, and I just wasn't thinking how it sounded."

"I-it's—it's all right, Dolly."

"Forget I said it, huh? Because I didn't mean a thing; just a manner of speaking. Hell, I knew all about you—everything there was to know in the beginning, didn't I? And it didn't make a damned bit of difference, did it?"

"I n-never wanted to, Dolly. With you, yes. Everything was different and I wanted to give you everything that I—"

"Sure. Don't you suppose I know that?" I smiled at her, gave her a big hug—and for a moment I forgot all about Joyce. "You're the sweetest, nicest girl in the world, and we're going to have a swell life together. We'll hang around town two or three weeks longer—just to make sure—and then we'll pull out. And there won't be any past, baby, just the future, and ... "

She snuggled up against me. After a while, I ran out of words, so I just held her and patted her. I kept it up for, well, maybe fifteen or twenty minutes. Then, a string of cars started to go by, and we had to move apart.

"Dolly. I hate to—I don't like to bother you, but—"

"You *couldn't* bother me," I said. "You just tell old Dolly about it, and if he can fix it up he will."

"Well, could I see you tonight? Just for a little while. I get so s-scared in that house! If I could see you for just a little while b-before I went to bed ... "

There was still some of the sickness and hurt in her eyes. Not a whole lot, but it wouldn't take much to make it into a lot. I couldn't have her think I was slapping her down again.

"Well, I'd sure like to," I said, "but it might not be too smart, see? If someone should spot me over there around your place—"

"Let me come over to yours, then! P-please, Dolly. Just for a few minutes and I won't ask you again until—until it's all over."

Well ...

Well?

"You weren't—you meant that about the police? You're sure they're not watching me? You're not afraid to have me—"

I said sure I was sure; I wouldn't snow her about a thing like that. "You see it's this way, honey. Here's the rub. My boss, this character Staples—the guy you took the bail money to—well, he drops out a lot in the evening. To talk about the work, you know. And if he saw you there, it would blow things higher than a kite. He was pretty suspicious about that dough, anyway. I wasn't supposed to have any, see, and you're sure not supposed to have any. We're not suppose to mean a thing to each other. So if he found out—"

She was nodding almost impatiently. She understood about Staples. But that still didn't take me off the hook.

"I could come later, Dolly. Any time—midnight. He wouldn't be there that late."

"Well, yeah, sure," I said. "But—uh—"

"Oh," she said, dully.

"Now, wait a minute," I said. "I'm trying to explain, honey. You see, well, it's kind of hard to put into words, but—uh—uh—"

"I understand," she said.

I couldn't have her feeling that way. It made me squirm, and it just wasn't safe. Not now. Not at this stage of the game, anyway, when she was still so shaky that she could hardly cast a shadow.

"Why don't we do this?" I said. "Suppose you come over around nine o'clock, and I'll meet you outside. I'll say—in case someone's there—I'll say that I want to get some cigarettes, and I'll meet you down the block there from the wrecking yard. On the corner there by the drug store."

"Well . . . If you're sure you want to."

"I'd love to. I just wanted to play it safe, see, that's all. Hell, baby, there's nothing I like better than being with you."

I made her believe it. I said I'd been worried about her being without dough, and I started to reach back to my sample case. And, then, I caught myself, and took out my wallet. I didn't want her to know I had the loot with me. The way she'd been feeling, just a little doubtful about me, she might decide to ask for a cut.

I gave her five bucks of my own money. We talked a little longer, and then I drove her to the bus stop and let her out.

I didn't feel like working that day, either, but I put in a few hours, just to pass the time. I took in around twenty dollars, padding it out with forty from the satchel. The rest of the day, I just fooled around; and at six I checked in.

Staples was okay. I mean, he didn't give me the needle. I was out of the store in ten minutes, and on my way home.

The gravel cars had been pulled off the siding, and three gondolas of coal were there tonight. One of the cars was sticking half way out into the street, and it was a close squeeze getting the car past it. I finally made it and I parked and went into the house.

I called out to Joyce. Her voice came back to me faintly from the bedroom. I glanced into the dinette.

Dinner was ready. It was on the table, but there was only one place setting. Mine.

I set down the sample case, took off my hat and coat. I hesitated, and then I went back to the bedroom. I paused in the doorway—it didn't seem like I could go any further—and stood looking in at her.

She was in bed with the covers pulled pretty well over her, but I could see she had on her nightgown. She was facing the wall, her back to me, and she didn't turn around.

"Y-you"—I cleared my throat—"You sick or something, honey?"

She didn't answer for a moment. Then, she said, her voice muffled, "I don't feel too well. Go and eat your dinner while it's hot, Dolly."

"Well, hell," I said. "Where are you sick, anyway? What's the matter?"

"Eat your dinner," she said—pretty crisply. "We can talk afterward."

"Well, okay," I said. "Maybe I'd better."

I didn't have much of an appetite for some reason, but I ate. I ate slow, taking my time, and I drank three cups of coffee afterwards. And when I couldn't hold any more coffee, I started smoking, lighting one cigarette after another.

She called to me.

I called back, "Yeah, I'll be there in a minute, honey."

I finished my cigarette. I got up and went down the hall toward the bedroom. And I got there. And I couldn't make myself go in. I said, "B-be . . . be with you in a minute, baby," and I went into the bathroom and closed the door.

I looked around in there, and it was like I'd never seen the place before. No, nothing had been changed, nothing had been done to it, but something had happened to me. Everything seemed strange, twisted out of shape. I was lost in a strange world, and there was nothing familiar to hang onto.

Nothing. No one. No one I could talk to, explain things to.

I sat down on the edge of the tub, and lighted a cigarette. I crushed it out in the sink without thinking; and then I got up and crumbled the butt into shreds and washed the shreds down the drain. I washed the sink out real good until there wasn't a spot or a stain left on it.

I sat down on the toilet, and lighted another cigarette.

I stayed there in the bathroom. It was a strange world, but it was even stranger outside. I could sit here and explain to myself, and hell, it was clear as daylight. But I couldn't explain to her.

She called to me.

I yelled that I'd be out in a minute ... and I stayed where I was.

She called again; I yelled again. She came to the door—finally—and knocked. And I yelled, for Christ's sake, what's the hurry, anyway? And she turned the knob and came in.

She'd been crying; so much and so long that she was cried out. And now her face was drawn, streaked with tears. But her yes were clear, and her voice was steady.

"I want to know, Dolly. I intend to know, so don't try to lie to me. Where did you get that money?"

THROUGH THICK AND THIN: THE TRUE STORY OF A MAN'S FIGHT AGAINST HIGH ODDS AND LOW WOMEN ... by Knarf Nollid

WELL, DEAR READER, in looking over my last installment I discovered that I have made a small error or two in fact. This was no fault of mine because, although I seldom complain, you have doubtless discovered that I am one hard luck son-of-a-bitch, and people keep pouring it on me until I don't know my tail from a t-bone. So this was the case in this case. There was so much happening at once that I got slightly balled up in my facts.

The truth is this—the truth about this girl, Mona, I was telling you about. This old woman she was living with, she wasn't actually her aunt at all. She was a kidnapper, see, and she'd kidnapped this poor girl from her wealthy parents while she was still no more than a tot—so naturally she didn't remember anything about them—and this one hundred thousand dollars was ransom money. The old woman was afraid to spend it because, well, hell, how do I know? Oh, yeah. She was afraid to spend it because at first she had to lay low until the heat was off, and after a while everyone got to believing that she didn't have a dime to her name and she *couldn't* spend it. It would have looked funny as hell, know what I mean? So that was the way it happened, or something like that. She couldn't bring herself to throw the dough away, but she couldn't spend it either. It was some sort of screwy deal like that, and however it was, it isn't really important. The important thing is that the money really belonged to Mona, since her wealthy parents had been dead many years of broken hearts. And since I had saved her from a fate worse than death, it wasn't any more than right that she should kind of let me take care of it for her. Or maybe even keep it all. Because if she was actually a tramp, like rumor said, I sure as hell wasn't going to have her tagging around with me.

Well, I was going to explain these true events to my wife, Joyce, when she returned unexpectedly and caught me with the dough. But I just couldn't think fast enough, I guess, so I stalled and a day or so later I told her I'd found the money. It sounded more logical than the truth, and anyway I hadn't been able to figure out the truth yet. Hell, how could I, the way things were popping at me right and left? This character Staples was giving me a hard time. Mona was giving me a hard time: worrying me about whether she was a tramp or not, and getting scared and making me scared. And, Joyce, well, I was glad she'd come back, because it looked like she'd turned over a new leaf and all was about to be well between us. But you can see how it was just one more goddamned thing to mix me up.

So I hadn't got around to tell her the truth yet. There wasn't any real incentive to, you know, as long as she believed that I'd found the money. Then the day came when she gave the house a good cleaning—and believe me it could stand it!—and when I get home that night, all knocked out after a rugged day of toil, she starts giving me a hard time. She hardly lets me finish my dinner before she starts yapping at me—wants me to come back in the bedroom and do some talking. So I rush through my meal and step in the bedroom for a minute—for God's sake, what's the world coming to when a guy can't go to the bathroom? But it seems like even this humble privilege is not to be mine.

I hardly have the door closed before she's calling to me. And I know something's plenty wrong, see, and all I want is time enough to figure out a good story. It's for her own sake, understand? Because if she decides I'm lying about the money, it leaves her in a pretty bad spot. She'll want me to go to the police or she'll go herself and I just can't allow that. Even though the money is rightfully mine. The cops won't believe the truth any more than she does, so . . . so, well you can see the situation.

I'm a pretty easy-going guy, and never hurt anyone in my life if I could get out of it. But if she tried to pin me down, give me a hard time when I already had more than I could stand, it would be just too bad for her.

So I stalled in the bathroom, wondering what the hell she'd found out and how the hell I could squirm out of it. But she just wouldn't have it that way; she wouldn't let me protect her. She had to bust into the bathroom on me, and ask where did I get the money. I told her. I said hell, honey, I already told you where I got it. And she said, you lied, Dolly. I must have known it right from the beginning, but I wanted so much to believe that—that—

"Where were you on Monday night, Dolly?"

"Monday night?" I said. "Oh, the night you came home. Why, I was out collecting, baby. I caught up with some long-time skips, and they paid off like—"

"They did not pay off. Because you weren't collecting."

"Now, wait just a minute," I said. "I told you about it at the time, told you exactly where I'd been. You saw the money I took in, and—"

"I saw you take some money out of that little bag and put it in your wallet. That was all you had, Dolly, except for a dollar or two. I could see that it was the next morning when you took the money I'd brought back from my trip."

I shrugged. I gave her the cold eye. Hell, what if I hadn't told her the whole truth? Was that any reason for her to break into the bathroom and accuse me of lying, and act like I'd committed a crime or something?

I will leave you to be the judge, dear reader.

All I will say is that, if you insist on putting yourself on a spot, pushing a man who has already been pushed too far, you have got to take the consequences.

"How well did you know Pete Hendrickson, Dolly?"

"Pete?" I said. "Pete Hendrickson? I never heard of him in my life."

"He was killed Monday night. He and a woman named Farrell."

"Yeah?" I said. "Oh, yeah. Seems like I remember reading something about it."

"You didn't know him personally?"

"Know him?" I laughed. "Why would I know a character like that?"

"You didn't know him?"

"I'm telling you," I said.

"Then why was he in this house? Why did he sleep

here?"

I gave her a look like I thought she was crazy. I wanted to protect her, see, and believe me I was doing everything I could. "Why, my God, honey," I said. "That's the screwiest thing I ever hear of! What ever gave you the idea that—?"

"This," she said. "I cleaned house today, and I found this. Down on the floor behind the bed."

She opened her hand, and held it out: a little blue and white card. Pete Hendrickson's social security card.

The stupid, sloppy bastard had slept with his clothes on that one night, and he'd let this slip out of his pocket. Just to give me a hard time later, sure. And—and what did it matter, anyhow? Look at the way he'd treated Mona; and besides that he was a Nazi or a Communist or—

"Why did you lie about it, Dolly? Why did you tell me you didn't know him?"

"Well, hell," I said, "I know a lot of people. I just didn't see that it made any difference."

"Were any of those other people here while I was away?"

"You think I'm running a hotel?" I said. "No, there wasn't anyone else here, and the only reason he was here was because I felt sorry for him and—uh—"

"Then he was with you Monday night, wasn't he? Monday evening before the murd—before it happened. There'd been someone with you; I could tell it the minute I stepped into the house. Two people had been here, drinking and smoking ... and if there wasn't anyone else ... "

"Baby," I said. "You're making a lot out of nothing. So what if he was here, what if it works out that I wasn't collecting that night? Don't you—"

"I want to know," she said. "That's what I want to know. Why you lied if it didn't matter."

"Don't you trust me?" I said. "Don't you love me? My God, maybe I did get a little mixed up and forget a few things, but—"

She moved away from me, shrugging my hands off her shoulders. "Why, Dolly? And where? Where were you Monday night, and where did you get that money?"

"Leave me alone," I said. "Goddammit, leave me alone!"

I didn't like to talk to her that way, understand, but why did she have to give me a hard time? And all over nothing.

"I'm waiting, Dolly."

"I already told you," I said. "I mean, maybe it wasn't the truth exactly. But that doesn't mean I did anything wrong. I am—m-my God, you act like you thought I'd killed those two people. Beat the old woman to death and shot Pete and ... Where you going? Where do you think you're going?"

"Oh, Dolly," she said. "H-how—what have you—"

I tried to tell her, then, what had happened. How things really were. How they could have been. And how did she know it wasn't true? How did she know that the old woman wasn't a kidnapper and that this money didn't belong to Mona's wealthy parents who had died years ago of broken hearts and ...

And she wouldn't even listen to me. She was tugging at the doorknob, staring at me with her eyes getting wider and wider like I was a goddamned maniac or something.

I made a grab for her, just trying to make her listen to reason you know. And for a moment I thought she was going to scream—yeah, call for help against her own husband—but she didn't. All she did was say—nothing. Nothing I remember. Not anything important.

It was an accident, of course. Hell, you know me, dear reader, and you are aware that I wouldn't hurt a goddamned fly if I could get out of it. I was just trying to grab her, to hold onto her while I made her listen to reason. But I grabbed pretty hard, I guess—sort of swung—and an unkind Fate decreed that the small understanding between us should end otherwise than happy ... TO BE CONTINUED (MAYBE).

...She said, "N-no, Dolly. Oh, n-no. I had to come back. I wanted to, anyway, but I had to. I was going to tell you as soon as everything was settled—"

"Everything's settled," I said. "It's damned good and settled."

"...don't know what you're doing! You can't, Dolly! N-no, please, NO! I'm pregnant!"

It was too late to stop. Anyway, how could I have stopped, even if it hadn't been too late?

I hooked her, and she went down in the bathtub. I bent over the tub, and ... And when I finally stripped off the nightgown and lifted her out, she didn't look like Joyce any more. Or anyone.

I carried her out the back door. I tossed her body up on the top of one of the coal cars, and climbed up after it. I dug down in the coal with my hands, scooping out a long shallow hole, and I buried her in that. Buried them.

IT WAS enough for one night. It was too much for a million nights, and I came back into the house feeling pretty good and relaxed. You understand. Nothing else could happen now, because everything had already happened. The worst. They couldn't throw anything more at me after this. They couldn't ever give me a bad time again.

It was too much, but now it was all over and they couldn't—

I came back into the house. I washed and cleaned up, thinking, thinking—just thinking—but not worrying.

They couldn't identify her. That train would be three days getting into Kansas City, and it stopped a half a dozen places between here and there. They wouldn't know where it had happened, when she'd been put onto the coal car, who she was. All I had to do was get rid of her clothes when I cleared out of here— and I'd be clearing out damned fast.

Because too much had already happened, and now nothing else could.

Mona could stay here with me tonight. Why not? The deal was on ice—nothing to worry about—and she was one swell kid. And I needed someone to be with me. I've always needed someone to be with me, and tonight—

So she'd stay here tonight, and in the morning I'd quit the store. Pick an argument with Staples and then tell him to go to hell, and walk out. And then Mona and I would take off, just the two of us and that good old hundred grand. It would be okay. There wasn't a hole in it any place, not on my side or hers. The county had ordered her to clear out of the house. No one could make anything out of it if she got out a little ahead of time.

We'd take off together, Joy—Mona—and me, and from then on, from now on ... Nothing more could happen.

I finished cleaning myself up and cleaning up the bathroom. I went out into the living room and had a good stiff drink. It seemed like it should have been awfully late, but it was only a little after eight-thirty. Almost twenty-five minutes before I was to meet Mona—before someone would be here with me.

I poured another stiff drink. I drank it, and I got to thinking it couldn't have happened—so much, so quickly—and if it couldn't, why it hadn't. And maybe I ought to take her back a little drink, since she wasn't feeling well. And I poured it out for her.

And drank it.

There was a knock on the door. I gave a little jump, and then I went to answer it; and, no, I didn't hesitate. Because there couldn't be anything more now, nothing ever again, and there was nothing to be afraid of.

I opened the door. Staples said, "Good evening, Frank," and I didn't answer—I couldn't answer—and he walked in past me.

"Well, Frank. You don't appear at all pleased to see me. Aren't you going to ask me to sit down?"

I shook my head. I said, "No. What the hell do you want, Stape?"

He sat down, crossing his fat little legs. "What do I want, Frank? We-el, let's say I'll be quite happy with pot luck. I'll take whatever you have."

20

HE COULDN'T mean what I thought he probably did. He couldn't know anything, and too much had already happened and . . . I sagged down in a chair across from his. It was the chair Pete had sat in, and he was in the place I had sat in when I was talking to Pete. I was in Pete's place, and he was in mine.

I started shaking my head. I didn't know what to say or do so I just shook my head.

"Yes," he said. "Oh, yes, Frank. Yes, indeed."

"No-no! I won't—" I broke off, made my voice steady. "What do you want? What are you talking about, anyway?"

And he laughed softly.

"Oh, Frank. You've been so clumsy, so obvious; such a thorough botch from the very beginning . . . Must we go into the tiresome details, or can't you see it for yourself?"

"I don't know what you're talking about," I said. "You h-hear? I don't—"

"Well," he sighed, "if we must, we must. I'll begin at the beginning and spell it out very slowly. Item . . ."

He held up a hand, then folded one of the chubby little fingers back into his palm. "Item one, Frank. On the day before your arrest for stealing company funds, you collected some thirty-eight dollars from the late Pete Hendrickson. On the same day you made a cash sale—or, rather, you turned in a cash-sale contract—in the amount of thirty-three dollars to one Mona Farrell. In the morning, then, on these two accounts, you should have checked in about seventy-one dollars. And frantic as you were to stave off arrest, you certainly would have turned it in, *if* you had had it. But you didn't; all you had was the money for the silverware. You used Pete's money, or most of it, to buy the girl a present."

"Now, wait a minute," I said. "That doesn't mean—you can't prove—"

"Prove?" His lips pursed thoughtfully. "Well, perhaps not, if we take it out of context, which, happily, I am not forced to do. At any rate, and at the moment, we are not discussing proof. I am merely pointing out your initial error, delving down to the center strand of that very ugly rope which you have hung around your neck.

"You gave the girl a thirty-three dollar present, and perhaps that is meaningless of itself. One more manifestation of a distorted personality. But it is not meaningless—it is not, my dear boy—when this same girl arrives at the store, and bails you out to the tune of more than three hundred dollars ... Or are you going to tell me that it wasn't the same girl?"

There was no use in denying it. I knew now who'd been watching her, who'd turned the car lights on her.

"All right," I said. "So I know her, I like her and she likes me. What of it? My wife skipped out and—"

"Please!" He held up his hand again. "I'm not at all interested in your morals. Nor in you personally, for that matter. Only in the money you obtained from what must be the two clumsiest murders on record."

He waited, waiting for me to deny it. And it wasn't any use, of course, but I did. "Money?" I said. "Murders? I don't know what you're—"

"Money. Murders," he nodded. "And, please, Frank, you're trying my patience. I don't know how you got next to the girl or how you managed to frame Pete, but I know that you did. The girl tipped you off to the fact that the old woman had a substantial sum of money. You—skipping over the gory details—you got it, and you still have it. Except for those amounts which you checked in as collections."

"Now, wait a—"

"Which you checked in as collections," he said firmly. "Would you like me to show it to you? I've laid it aside just in case you became stubborn. Approximately a dozen bills, supposedly collected from an assorted group of people but with their serial numbers in sequence. You got it, Frank, and you got a very substantial sum. Nothing less would have tempted you to take such a terrible risk, and Ma Farraday was just the woman to have had a hefty chunk of cash."

"But—Ma Farraday?" I said.

"Mmmm. Do you recall my telling you that I'd been to visit an old friend? That was Ma—better known locally as Mrs. Farrell. I went to see her in the morgue after my suspicions about you became aroused. Once I recognized her, I was certain that—but I see you don't recognize the name?"

He waited again, one eyebrow cocked upward. Then, he grinned and went on:

"A little before your time, I imagine, but the Farraday gang was notorious in the Southwest some twenty to twenty-five years ago. Bank robbers. Ma and her three sons. Ma doing the planning, and the three men faithfully carrying out her orders. Three of the orneriest, coldest-blooded killers ever to shoot a teller in the back. And their wives and children—they all lived together near the town where I worked—their wives and children were just as ornery as they were. Why—Yes, Frank?"

"N-nothing," I said. "I mean, I thought ... "

"I know. I was confident that your interest in the oil business and my early days in Oklahoma was something more than casual. But, no, there was no oil on the Farraday property; they lived too far back in the hills. For that matter, I doubt that even had they owned oil-producing land, it would have altered their way of life a whit. They were cruel, vicious, because they wanted to be. It was all they understood—men, women and children. Being a very clannish lot, with little trust in the law, their neighbors protected and put up with them for years. In the end, however, they finally became so outraged that they moved in and massacred the lot of them. Shot them like the swine they were, then burned their dwellings. Wiped out the entire family—supposedly."

Mona. She was part of an outfit like that. No wonder she'd been so ready to kill her own aunt—her grandmother, probably. No wonder that she acted like—

"I said *supposedly,* Frank. Criminal investigation was just emerging from swaddling clothes in those days and, of course, neither Ma nor the various children had police records. A number of bodies were found in the smoldering ruins; also the charred remnants of a quantity of currency. Ergo, and in the absence of proof to the contrary, it was assumed—*believed,* I should say—that the entire family was wiped out, and with them their ill-gotten gains. But you and I know better, don't we, Frank? We are the only ones who do know."

He winked at me, grinning with his puffy little lips drawn back from his teeth. Like a cat that's just had a good meal. He licked his lips slightly, grinning and waiting, and my stomach turned over and over. And the band grew tighter and tighter around my head.

I began to tremble. My mouth opened and I felt a scream crawling up from my throat, and I had to swallow hard to choke it back.

"N-no!" I said. "You've got it all wrong, Stape! I—"

"Dear, dear," he said. "Oh, dear me. You are such a tiresome fellow, Frank."

"I'm telling you! It's the God's truth, Stape. The girl was kidnapped, see. She was actually the daughter of a very wealthy family, and the money was ransom money and—and—"

He laughed out loud. "And you were going to act as custodian of it, eh? Oh, my dear boy, I'm almost embarrassed for you."

"It's true, goddammit!" *It had to be true. Something had to be true besides what—what was true.* "That's why the old woman didn't spend any of the money, see? She found out it was marked, and—"

"But it wasn't marked, Frank. I know it. You must know it also, unless you're a much bigger fool than you appear."

"Well-uh-well, then, she found out—she figured out—that the serial numbers had been recorded, and—"

"Oh? Then why, since it was unspendable, did she keep it all these years?"

He was playing with me, laughing at me, having a hell of a time for himself. "Yes, Frank? And why—if the authorities are on the lookout for those serials— why aren't you in custody?"

"Well—" I had to go on. I was talking crap, making

a horse's ass of myself, but I had to go on. "Well, there's bound to be something wrong with it. If there wasn't, why didn't she spend it? Why did she go on living like a goddamned hog when—"

"Because she was one, a grasping old sow."

"You don't know," I said. "You don't know that the money isn't hot. She could have found out that—"

"Then, why, as I asked a moment ago, didn't she destroy it?"

"Well—uh—well, because she couldn't! Jesus, you've got a hun—a pretty good wad of dough, how *can* you destroy it? I couldn't. She couldn't. So she just hung onto it, figuring that maybe some day, somehow, she might be able to shove it—"

"Oh, Frank ... "

"You don't know," I said. "Goddammit, you can't be sure, Stape!"

"I not only can be, but I am. You see, I had some several dealings with the Farradays at this store I managed. Delivered merchandise to their mountain retreat at considerably above the market prices. There was nothing criminal about our association— nothing provably illegal, I should say—but the company became embarrassed to the point of transferring me to another town ... However! Enough of personal history. My point is that the Farradays were strictly bank robbers."

"But they might have pulled one kid—"

"Stop it! No more nonsense, Frank ... How much did you get and where is it?"

I looked down at the floor. I looked up again, keeping my eyes away from the corner where the sample case was.

"She didn't have as much as I thought. Just ten thousand dollars. I can—well, I got it out in the country, see—but I can bring it in the morning."

"Ten thousand? You mean, a hundred thousand, I'm sure. You almost said it a moment ago."

"All right," I said. "So goddammit, there's a hundred thousand. Come on with me and we'll go and get it."

He hesitated. Then he nodded, smiling faintly. "Very well, Frank, but perhaps I should tell you something first. I left a letter with the night clerk at my hotel—a very reliable man, incidentally. He's instructed to mail it if I fail to return by midnight."

His smile spread, and he laughed out loud again.

I thought, *It can't be like this* ... And I guess I must have said it.

"But it is, Frank; it is like that. And now you will produce the money. Immediately!"

I got up. I brought the case over to the coffee table and snapped it open. I started to reach in for the satchel, digging it out from under the samples, and he brushed my hands away and grabbed it himself.

He opened it. He made a funny purring sound.

"Mmmm. Wonderful ... I hope you won't think I'm greedy if I don't offer to share with you?"

"You've got to," I said. I kept saying it. "You got to, Stape. A—a few grand, well, one grand. Something! Anything! I ki—I did it all, and—"

"So sorry." He shook his head. "But I'll be happy to give you a word of wisdom. You have no problems which money will solve."

"You son-of-a-bitch," I said.

"You really don't, Frank. You'd be just as miserable with the money as without it ... Well, much as I hate to leave such pleasant company ... "

He buttoned his coat, and stood up. He tucked the money satchel under his arm.

"I want that silverware contract back," I said. "By

God, you'll never be able to hold that over me."

"The sil—oh, yes, to be sure. And very shrewd of you. You can pick it up in the morning, get your wages to date at the same time."

"My wages," I said.

"Well? No more questions? You're not wondering why I delayed calling you to account until tonight?"

"Get out," I said.

"The girl, dear boy: the clinching bit of proof. I didn't really need it, but—"

"Get out!"

"Of course. But shouldn't you invite her in, Frank? She's just around the corner ... and you do look so lonesome."

21

LONESOME, he said. The man said I looked lonesome. And I had all kinds of company. All kinds. All dead. All jumping up in front of me wherever I looked, all laughing and crying and singing in my mind.

All dead. And all for nothing.

All for a dame that had been born rotten, and got more rotten every damned day of her life.

... I met her, and brought her back to the house. I told her about Staples and losing the money. I laid it out cold for her, kind of hoping, you know, that she'd bitch or give me a hard time about it. But she didn't let out a peep. She was sympathetic, sorry on my account, but she acted like it didn't matter to her. As long as she could be with me, that was all that mattered.

I began to think that maybe I might be mistaken about her. To feel that she was the swell kid I'd thought she was in the beginning. It was pretty hard to swallow, and, of course, I couldn't sell myself completely. But I did it enough. Enough to keep from slugging her. Enough to put up with her ... for the time being.

She was all I had, you see; all I'd got for all I'd done. And I had to have someone with me. I'd almost always had someone with me.

I went out and got some more whiskey—it took just about my last nickel. I came back and we talked and drank. And after a while she talked and I drank. And pretty soon there was no more talk, and only me drinking.

She fell asleep with her head in my lap. I passed out. When morning came, we were still there on the lounge.

I fixed us some coffee and toast—I didn't want her slopping around with *my* grub. I told her to beat it back to her house and gather up anything she wanted to take with her. She left, hurrying, and I went back into the bedroom.

I stuffed all of Joyce's things into a big pasteboard carton. Clothes, cosmetics and toilet articles: everything. I carried the box out into the alley, and set it down by the trash can. Then, I drove down to the store.

The other collectors had checked out, and Staples was alone. He gave me the silverware contract and I struck a match to it, dropping it to the floor and kicking the ashes to pieces.

"Such a messy fellow," he pouted. "But, I suppose, I shouldn't chide you ... Your money, Frank. I'm making it a full fifty dollars."

I picked up the money, not saying anything. I gave him a slow, hard stare; and then I turned around and started to leave.

"Frank—" There was a worried note in his voice. "What—uh—what are your plans, Frank?"

"What's that to you?" I said.

"But I've always been concerned for you, dear boy. Always. And it's dawned on me that since you'll doubtless want to be moving on ... "

I began to get it. He *was* worried. He wasn't just another hired hand that could pull out without a moment's notice. The books would have to be audited and the stock inventoried before he could leave; and that would take two or three weeks at the inside. And he didn't like the idea of me being in town during that time. I might get desperate, see? Might get drunk and jam myself up with the police ... and do a little talking.

"I don't know," I said. "Why would I want to travel? I figure I'll stay right here."

He gave me a peeved look, but he opened the cash drawer. He took out all the currency inside, counted it and shoved it through the wicket.

"Four hundred and forty-seven dollars, Frank. Almost five hundred with the fifty you have. That should see you well on your way."

"I like it here," I said. "I'm not going anywhere."

"Now, Frank ... "

"Not unless you do a lot better than that," I said. "Hell, make it a grand, anyway. With all you've got—"

"But I don't have it with me. It's put away in a safe place, and it's going to remain there until my resignation takes effect."

"Well ... well," I said. "Write me a check, then. Give me your check for five hundred."

"Oh, ... " He shook his head, grinning. "Must you really be so obvious? ... No checks. I couldn't oblige you even if I was stupid. It will take just about my entire bank balance to square with the cash drawer."

I was sure he was lying, but there wasn't much I could do about it. He was just a little worried—not actually scared—and I'd played that worry for all it was worth.

I picked up the money, and left.

... I owed two hundred and thirty on the car. I paid it off—I couldn't have a goddamned finance company on my tail—and went back to the house. Mona was there waiting for me. I got my stuff together, and loaded all our baggage into the car. There was quite a bit of it, since I figured I'd better take Joyce's. It wasn't monogramed and it was pretty good stuff, and it might look funny if I left it behind.

I'd always made out pretty well in Omaha. As well, I mean, as I've made out anywhere. So that's where I headed for, and we got there just after dark. We stopped at a diner for a bite to eat. The waitress brought me a newspaper. I glanced at it ... and that was our last stop in Omaha.

I started driving again, and I drove almost night and day. To Des Moines. Down across to Grand Island. Across to Denver ... I sold the car in Denver, a lousy three hundred and twenty-five bucks, and we started traveling by bus.

Yeah, I suppose she wondered what the score was. Or maybe she didn't either. She hadn't been around enough to know when something was screwy and when it wasn't, so maybe she didn't wonder. Anyway, she didn't ask any questions, try to give me a hard time. And it was a damned good thing for her that she didn't.

I'd had it, brother, know what I mean? And it looked like I was going to keep right on getting it. Because Staples had given the cops a bum steer—tole 'em I had a seaman's ticket and probably intended to ship out—but that didn't help much. Nothing helped much. The crew haircut, the horn-rimmed glasses, the mustache. I was still scared as hell, afraid to settle down in one place.

It was lousy, the lousiest stinking luck a guy ever had in his life. It—goddammit, it just wasn't fair! I ask you, now, did you ever hear of coal being moved by anything but regular freight? You're damned right you didn't and neither did anyone else. But that one car—that one car—they had to make an exception out of it. It got hooked onto a manifest, an express freight, and it didn't stop until it got into Kansas City. It was in there at noon the next day, and they started unloading it right away—they couldn't wait, goddamn them. And inside of an hour, the police doctor was posting the body.

Well, that soon, it was easy to fix the time of death. And they knew the body couldn't have been put on the train but one place. So they wired the cops at that place, and the cops started sniffing around, and they found that box of stuff back in the alley by the trash can ...

I had to keep moving. My money was running out, and I had to keep moving; and if I hadn't been saddled with her—chained to a goddamned tramp—

Well.

Well, she finally started in on me. I didn't have it tough enough, I guess, so she had to make it tougher. Watching me all the time like I was a goddamned freak or something. Not saying anything unless I spoke to her. You know: a lot of little things. Wearing me down little by little.

And stupid! The only thing she could do was bawl, and she never missed a chance at that.

I was walking a little ahead of her that day in Dallas. I'd told her for God's sake, if she wanted to look and act like a goddamned tramp she could walk by herself. So I was ahead of her, like I say, and finally

I looked around; and she wasn't there any more. Hardly anyone was on the sidewalk any more.

They were all out on the street about a half block back, crowded around the front of a big truck ...

UPWARD AND ONWARD: THE TRUE STORY OF A MAN'S FIGHT AGAINST HIGH ODDS AND LOW WOMEN ... by Derf Senoj

I WAS BORN in New York City of poor but honest parents, and from my earliest recollections I was out working and trying to make something of myself. But from my earliest recollections someone was always trying to give me a hard time. It was that way with everything I did. One way or another, I'd get the blocks put to me; so I will mercifully spare you the sordid details.

I kept thinking that if I had some little helpmeet to dwell with, the unequal struggle would not be so unequal. But I didn't have any more luck that way than I did in the other. Tramps, that's all I got. Five goddamned tramps in a row ... or maybe it was six or seven, but it doesn't matter. It was like they were all the same person.

Well, finally I landed in Oklahoma City, and it looks like at last my luck has changed. Not with money. I was buying the gold, door to door, and how can you make any money when everybody cheats you? But it looked like it had sure changed with women. It not only looked that way, but it was that way. And as far as the money went, she had enough for forty people.

I met her when I was working this swell apartment house there in the City. I sneaked in past the doorman, and hers was the first apartment I hit. Classy? Beautiful? Well, all I can say is that I'd never seen anything like her. I could hardly believe it when she smiled and asked me inside.

I was ashamed to hit her up on the gold. I said I was looking for a party that used to live there, and so on, and I was sure sorry to have bothered her. And—

"Now, now—" She laughed, but she didn't laugh at me, understand. It was nice and sympathetic. "Don't apologize for your job. Of course, I am a little disturbed to see a gentleman of your personality and evident ability doing this kind of—"

"Well," I said, "it's just temporary, see? I got a little down on my luck, and I had to take what I could get."

"How dreadful! You sit right down and I'll fix you a nice drink."

I sat down on about two thousand dollars worth of lounge. She brought our drinks, and sat down next to me. She smiled at me and kept the conversation going, because naturally I was pretty speechless.

I finished my drink and started to get up. She put her hand on my arm. "Please," she said. "Please don't go. I've been so lonely since my husband died."

I said I was certainly sorry to hear of her husband's death. Her eyes clouded up a little for a moment, and then she shook her head. "It's lonely without him and n-naturally I didn't want him to die, b-but—but, oh, it's a terrible thing to say but I think I'd actually begun to hate him! He misrepresented himself. He pretended to be everything I wanted, and then after we were married ... "

"I know what you mean," I said. "I know exactly what you mean, ba—uh—"

"Say it," she whispered, and she turned and threw her arms around me. "Say I'm your baby. Say it, say anything to me, do anything to ... you like. But j-just don't go away ... "

And it was like a beautiful dream, dear reader, but I'm
talk about dreams
kidding you negative: that was exactly how I came to meet the lovely Helene, my princess charming. Thus, at last, were two love-hungry souls united.

You will notice that I haven't described her, but I can't. Because she looked so many different ways. When she went out where anyone else could see her, she always looked the same way: the way she looked that first day I met her. But when we were alone, well, if I hadn't known it was her sometimes, I wouldn't have known it was her
a goddamned syphilitic bag
the same woman. She had dozens of different complete outfits—clothes that a girl of eighteen would wear, or a woman of twenty-five, or thirty-five and so on. All complete from house dresses to evening gowns. And she had all of these different kinds of make-up. Powder and lipstick and rouge—dozens of different shades—hairpieces and eyelashes and brows and teethcaps. Even little glass things to slip in over her eyes and change their color. It was kind of a hobby with her, see, making herself up in all those different ways. And right at the start it made me a little uneasy; I got to wondering what was real and what wasn't: And maybe if I saw her as she really
one more bag like all the rest
was, I wouldn't be able to take it. But that was just at

first. You see it could be no other way, dear reader: I mean, she had to be
a bag in a fleabag, for Christ's sake, and I couldn't go any
beautiful and classy and all that a man desires in a woman. All the royal rooking I'd got from tramps, I couldn't take any more. And after the long unequal struggle I had at least found my heart's desire.

She'd inherited a pile of dough from her father; but that's
stole her brother-in-law's savings
about all I ever found out about her or him. I never even learned his name—her maiden name. She acted embarrassed when I mentioned anything about her background, so I didn't do it more than a time or two. I figured that the old man had probably made his pile selling clap medicine or something like that, and naturally she was embarrassed. And it was best to stay off the subject. After all, although I had always worked my can off and never complained, there were a few chapters in my own life which I preferred to remain sealed.

Her money was in a bank in another city—just where I
hidden in the mattress
don't know. But she was so embarrassed about her maiden name that she never cashed any checks there in town, or let the bank send her any dough. Whenever she ran short, she'd just hop a plane to this city and draw out what she wanted, and be back the same night.

She'd gone after some dough, the morning this story broke in the newspapers—a story about some people I used to know. And I

wow! the wine and the hay! yeeoweeeee
laughed so goddamned hard when I read it that I
almost busted a rib. I read it and re-read it, all day
long, and each time I laughed
safe now. safe with a bag in a fleabag
harder than ever:

The 20-year-old Stirling kidnap case appeared to be
solved today with the arrest of an ex-store manager
and admitted associate of the notorious Farraday
gang.

The suspect is H.J. Staples, 55. More than $90,000
of the $100,000 ransom money was recovered from his
swank Sarasota, Fla., hotel suite.

Staples first came under scrutiny of the authorities
about four months ago when several hundred dollars
in kidnap currency was deposited to the account of a
store he then managed. Believing that the deposit was
made as a "feeler," law officials refrained from
arresting him until he put large and thoroughly
incriminating sums into circulation.

Ramona Stirling was the only child of multi-
millionaire oil-man, Arthur Stirling, and his semi-
invalid wife. Three years old at the time, Ramona was
snatched from the grounds of the family's luxurious
Tulsa estate, after her nurse had been lured into the
house by a fake telephone call.

The ransom of $100,000 was demanded, and
promptly paid. But an inexperienced newscaster
revealed that the serial numbers of the currency had
been recorded. With the divulging of this information,
the Stirlings lost all contact with the kidnapers, and it
is generally conceded that the child was murdered.

Mrs. Stirling died less than six weeks after the

kidnaping. Her husband went to his grave the following month. In the absence of heirs, the great Stirling fortune was claimed by the state.

The suspect Staples quit his job some three months ago and began traveling about the country, making various small expenditures along the way. At last convinced, apparently, that time had cooled off the "hot" money, he arrived in Florida yesterday and began to splurge. His arrest followed.

Grilled by state, federal and local officials, he told a wildly implausible story of how he came into possession of the money. Full details are not yet available but it is known that his tale involved "Ma" Farraday (of the aforementioned gangsters) and Frank Dillon, a former associate of Staples', who had been sought for several months in connection with the death of his wife and their unborn child. Officials place no credence whatsoever in the suspect's "explanations."

That Staples was once on excellent terms with the gangsters is acknowledged. It is pointed out, however, that the entire Farraday family was wiped out more than two decades ago; and that, this being the case, Staples' statement that Dillon killed "Ma" for the ransom money is nothing short of ridiculous. Moreover, it was pointed out, the Farradays were bank robbers. They were never known to have indulged in any other criminal activity, and it is virtually unbelievable that they would have.

As for Dillon, authorities now believe that he was himself a murder victim and he is no longer being sought as a fugitive. They theorized that he and Mrs. Dillon somehow learned that Staples had the ransom cash, and that the latter killed both. Dillon's body, it was explained, could have been buried in a coal car which was destined for a conveyor-fed blast furnace ...

I laughed and laughed when I read that story. I felt
safe. from what? not the thing I needed to be safe from.
good all day. And then evening came on, and I didn't laugh
and it was just like always only worse. the worst tramp
any more and I didn't feel good anymore. Because it was
of all, the worst fleabag of all. and I couldn't take it.
quite a tragedy, when you got to thinking about it: and I
the end had to be better than this. so we drank the wine.
guess you know dear reader I'm a pretty soft-hearted son-
we smoked the hay. we started sniffing the snow. they
of-a-bitch. Yes, it was a terrible tragedy and whoever was
say you can't do it. guzzle the juice and puff the mary
responsible for it ought to be jailed. Making a guy want
and sniff the c. but we did. we did that and then we went
what he couldn't get. Making him so he couldn't get much,
on the h. we started riding the main line. we got sick as
but he'd want a lot. Laying it all out for him every place
bastards but we kept right on and after a while, man oh, man,
he turned—the swell cars and clothes and places to live.
we didn't know from nothing. we were blind, too paralyzed
Never letting him have anything, but always making him want.
to feel, too numb. but everything began to get beautiful.
Making him feel like a bastard because he didn't have what
she was and the room was and I was. it was like it ought
he couldn't get. Making him hate himself, and if a guy
to be at the end if it's never been that way before. and
hates himself how can he love anyone else? Helene came home,
we kept digging into the mattress, and the porter kept
my fairy princess, and she saw I was feeling low so she fixed
bringing in the stuff. helene started vomiting a lot, but
me a big drink. And right after that I began to get drowsy.
it didn't seem to bother her and it didn't bother me any.
I knew everything that was going on, I could hear and talk,
even the puke was beautiful like everything else. she was the
I was really wide awake. But still I was sleepy; and if

most beautiful woman in the world and all I wanted was to do
that doesn't make sense I can't help it. I went and
something nice for her, show her how much I appreciated and
stretched out on the bed, and she came in and sat beside
loved her. and I didn't have but the one thing, the only thing,
me. She had a big pair of shears in her hand, and she sat
I guess, I ever gave a woman. it was all I had, all I'd ever had
snipping the ends of her hair, staring down at me. And I
to give. and I was afraid she might not want it but I had to
looked at her, my eyes dropping shut. And she made herself
make the offer. she was all the women of the world rolled
look like Joyce and then like Mona, and then . . . all the others.
into one. so it was the very least I could do, and I'd have to do
She said I'd disappointed her; I'd turned out like all her
it fast. she was in the bathroom puking. I got up and shoved
other men. You deceived me, she said. You're no different
my foot through the window. it woke me up a little; the cold
from the rest, Fred. And you'll have to pay like the rest.
air, and those jagged splinters of glass. but I probably
I'm drugged, ain't I? I said. Oh, yes, she said. You won't
wouldn't feel anything, the load I was carrying. and she was
feel a thing, and when you wake up it will all be over.
entitled to it. and anyway I wasn't going to need it any
There'll be nothing more to worry about. Won't that be
longer. it was all over and there was no use in hanging
wonderful, Fred, don't you want me to, darling. I nodded
onto that. I pulled off my clothes, what was left of them, and
and she began unfastening and fumbling and then, then,
poked my leg through the window. I straddled it, sawing
she lowered the shears. She began to use the shears, and
rocking back and forth, and it didn't take hardly any time
then she was smiling again and letting me see. There, she
at all. helene came to the door of the bathroom, and she
said, that's much better, isn't it? And, then, nice as I'd

184

didn't want it, all I had to give. she began laughing, screaming.
been, she started laughing. Screaming at me.
I threw myself out the window.

About the Author

James Meyers Thompson was born in Anadarko,
Oklahoma, in 1906. He began writing fiction at a very
young age, selling his first story to *True Detective*
when he was only fourteen. In all, Jim Thompson wrote
twenty-nine novels and two screenplays (for the
Stanley Kubrick films *The Killing* and *Paths of Glory*).
Films based on his novels include: *Coup de Torchon
(Pop. 1280), Serie Noire (A Hell of a Woman), The
Getaway, The Killer Inside Me, The Grifters*, and
After Dark, My Sweet. A biography of Jim Thompson
will be published by Knopf.